PRAISE FOR ANITA FE

ANITA FELICELLI'S *HOW WE K₁*

"A story collection about the costs of the way we move through time, both collectively—sweeping toward the climate disaster that's rendered gorgeously and devastatingly here—and individually. The characters in How We Know Our Time Travelers build themselves clay children, holograms of their dead families, and whole armies of automatons based on long-vanished girlfriends, and they invent elixirs of eternal life and time machines, all in an effort to revise the definitive moments of their lives. Felicelli's particular magic animates this longing and makes us feel it too."

—Clare Beams, author of *The Garden*

"*How We Know Our Time Travelers* is aching and wondrous, full of longing for what could have been, as well as an insatiable hunger for what little we have now. From near futures about to be washed away in a deadly tide, to a present world shrouded in the smoke of distant wildfires, Felicelli's stories sing the world electric and mourn its destruction from the edge of the precipice."

—Elizabeth Gonzales James, author of
The Bullet Swallower and *Mona at Sea*

"Reading each of the stories in *How We Know Our Time Travelers* feels like sliding a finger along a knife's edge. If human life on this planet one day ends, and future earth-dwellers want to know what the dying days felt like, I can imagine them rescuing this sharp and daring book from some burnt-out library and, upon reading it, finally understanding what it was we did to ourselves, and how, even as we were doing it, we wished so hard that things could be different."

—Vauhini Vara, Pulitzer Prize finalist and author of
The Immortal King Rao and *This is Salvaged*

"With deftness, wisdom, and the beauty of artful language, Anita Felicelli's masterful stories herald what life has become in our new reality of robots, holograms, climatic disasters, and biospheric damage. Empathetic to the aching loneliness of humans while highlighting our capacity for greater intimacies and our bending of time whether in romance, technology engagement, dementia, delusion, or staring down death—this dazzling collection *How We Know Our Time Travelers* will never leave you, because the future is here."

—Lisa Teasley, author of *Glow in the Dark* and *Fluid*

"Felicelli's power resides in her capacity to ground us and awe us with thrilling simultaneity. She's chiseling out a new genre called Existential Dystopia that celebrates the beauty and bruises of being alive."

—Joshua Mohr, author of *Model Citizen*

"Haunting, powerful, and eerily prescient, Felicelli's surreal new collection is essential reading for our volatile age. From decade-jumping street kids dodging steam tunnel apparitions to an app-happy couple carelessly gamifying their relationship, her unforgettable characters grapple with memory, technology, and time itself as they face down a terrifying future, one hounded at every turn by ghosts of the past."

—Emily Holleman, author of *Cleopatra's Shadows*

"A luminous and poignant collection. Anita Felicelli writes with a deep intelligence and longing. These stories linger with you long after the last page."

—Akil Kumarasamy, author of *Meet Us by the Roaring Sea*

ANITA FELICELLI'S *CHIMERICA*

"Felicelli's remarkable Chimerica is a coolly surrealist legal thriller—in turns sly, absurd, emotionally vivid, and satirically incisive—that shifts the reader into a world just adjacent to our own."

—Jonathan Lethem

"Felicelli blends the matter-of-fact with the mysterious in this utterly unique and compellingly readable debut. *Chimerica* is more than the story of a woman coming into her own power; it's a keen dive into the worlds of law, visual art, and marriage. You really couldn't ask for a novel with better ingredients. Did I mention there's a talking lemur? THERE'S A TALKING LEMUR."

—Kelly Luce

"Anita Felicelli's propulsive debut novel, *Chimerica*, almost dares you to try to categorize it. . . . perhaps most of all, it's a work of cannily revisionist California noir, a genre that, in Felicelli's deft hands, somehow encompasses all the others, reflecting the world we think we know back to us in all its strangeness."

—*Los Angeles Review of Books*

"A fantastic, fantastical book."

—*The Millions*

"Anita Felicelli's debut novel is a magical ride through time and place with a talking lemur."

—*Ms. magazine*

"A brilliant and subversive transnational ridicule of the American legal thriller genre."

—*MetroSilicon Valley*

ANITA FELICELLI'S *LOVE SONGS FOR A LOST CONTINENT*

"Felicelli's best stories are her boldest."

—Rumaan Alam, *New York Times*

"Felicelli creates a kind of conversation with the reader, allowing one to submerge into her fictional worlds and then return to the surface with new understandings about the world we live in today."

—*San Francisco Chronicle*

"Felicelli's storytelling often starts out in a deceptively benign manner before plunging into sudden depths. Her language is mostly restrained and subtle so that the big moments are not so much about explosive drama as about essential revelations."

—*PopMatters*

"This shining debut collection of short stories from Anita Felicelli centers Tamil Americans, touching on themes of identity, magic and everyday life, love in different forms, and the history of one's own roots."

—*The Margins*

"It tackles the difficulty of living in the in-between, in the interstices of identities, and the often deeply flawed way human beings deal with this liminality and confusion."

—*Los Angeles Review of Books*

"Love Songs for a Lost Continent revels in the murky in-between spaces where the monstrous intersects with the benign and something essential is revealed."

—*Foreword Reviews*

"Somber but undeniably affecting and profound tales."

—*Kirkus Reviews*

"This is a book we needed to read yesterday; this is a book we will still be reading tomorrow."

—Porochista Khakpour

"An expansive, inventive meditation on the shifting landscape of identity, on how people can be shaped and reshaped by violence and power and love. Anita Felicelli has a singular eye for the moments that transfigure lives, and this tremendous debut collection announces the arrival of a stunning new voice."

—Laura van den Berg, author of *The Third Hotel*

"These stories probe the limits of love, the fluidity of home, and the pressures and resistance of women in a patriarchal landscape without ever losing humor, engagement, and a quiet elegance and tenderness."

—Chris Abani, author of *The Secret History of Las Vegas* and *The Face, Cartography of the Void*

"Anita Felicelli will hook her arm into yours and run with you through an India, an America, a history and future that ring with truth and radical growth."

—Shanthi Sekaran, author of *Lucky Boy* and *The Prayer Room*

HOW WE KNOW OUR TIME TRAVELERS

HOW WE KNOW OUR TIME TRAVELERS

Stories

Anita Felicelli

wtaw press

SANTA ROSA, CALIFORNIA

Copyright © 2024 Anita Felicelli

All rights reserved. No part of this publication may be reproduced or transmitted in any form or by any means without written permission from the publisher, except in the case of brief excerpts or quotes embedded in reviews, critical essays, or promotional materials where full credit is given.

This is a work of fiction. Names, characters, places, and incidents are either the product of the author's imagination or are used fictitiously.

Library of Congress Control Number: 2024937440

Edited by Peg Alford Pursell
Designed by Mike Corrao

How we know our time travelers / Anita Felicelli.
ISBN: 979-8-9877197-7-0 (pbk) | 979-8-9877197-8-7 (epub)

Published by WTAW Press
PO Box 2825
Santa Rosa, CA 95405

"Perhaps we always want the person we love to have the existence of a ghost."

—Adolfo Bioy Casares, *The Invention of Morel*

To the ice cream man I met many years ago.

CONTENTS

UNTIL THE SEAS RISE

O N THE NIGHT OF THE big wave, we ignore the warnings blowing up our phones and stay on the beach. It's Violet's idea, of course it is. Whether we're smoking weed at midnight in the yellow sour grass by the gas station or drinking Kahlúa-and-ice-cream shakes on the clock or skimming money off the top of the cash register at work, it's always, always Violet's idea to break rules. And when it's her idea, we never get caught. She's good at breaking rules, at finding tiny nooks and crannies between words, inside words to figure out where you can slip through, at finding the inconsistencies between what someone might have said and what they probably meant, or what you could argue they intended. Back when we were still in school together, Dad would shake his head and say anyone who broke rules with such sophisticated elán would someday be a lawyer or a criminal. Well, guess which one she chose.

On Tuesdays, I work a different shift from Violet at the co-operative grocery on the streets above Nye Beach, five to one, and it's a rough shift because produce comes in later that day, which means I have to hustle to get it shelved. With the everlasting drought, farmers are having trouble securing an adequate supply of water for their greenhouses. Outside, the surface of soil has changed, irrevocably, because of how blazing hot it gets in the summer, so they keep building these greenhouses with rich, dark dirt like we used to have. Crops have been emerging paler, wheat and eggplants the color of ghosts—and blander too. Popular podcast hosts and their guests have started to mention what was once a fringe notion: developing a technology to produce all food synthetically now that we've rocketed past the point of stopping the death of the planet. Now that we've neared the precipice. There are warnings on these podcasts, too, not to trust a strange cult movement that has developed around fog catching, once an obscure little hobby, now the center of focus for a desperate community, many of them nomads who spend their time on the coast despite the sea rise, and who believe in overthrowing the government in order to turn the clock back on our environment. The gold bell over the door jingles, and I glance up from the tray of emaciated tomatoes. Violet arriving at the store for the start of her shift just as I'm done restocking.

Late, Violet! I say as she waltzes in. She shrugs, and even her shrug is elegant. She looks beautiful, always does, her raven-black hair slicked back tight with gel in a ballerina bun, her face starry with pierces, tiny hoops, her lips streaked a shimmery red. There's a sadness, too, in her eyes, and it's the sadness that holds me back from scolding her—ever. Since her mother died in the wildfires a year ago—one of the worst wildfires in history, though if we're honest, which we're not, they're all bad— shadows have spread under her eyes, giving her a perpetually haunted look, like she's expecting death to come calling for her, any day now, or like maybe she's calling death to her.

Oh, you know. She holds up her hands, palms up. I'm thinking we should go out to the beach. Bonfire tonight? Sunset? We'll roast marshmallows, smoke out, get crunk. How we used to do in high school?

I shake my head. She always remembers beach bonfires as exquisitely romantic, but the shore was a six-hour drive from our hometown after school, and the air turned freezing cold on the beach at night. Still, the starshine made you feel like the world was going to be all right, even though to hear the news it clearly wasn't, it was worsening every day. The wind whipped up so hard and loud you could barely hear each other, and no amount of Fuzzy Navels, no bonfire could ever warm you up out there on the sand.

Why don't we just rent a movie and invite everyone over? There's this Swedish horror movie we talked about getting from the library last time.

Come on, she says. It's been years! And how many of those depressing foreign films can you watch in this lifetime? Do you want me to kill myself?

All right, yeah, we don't want that. I say it reluctantly but try to smile.

She does this, you know? Turns everything into the most dramatic version of itself. Makes even the tiniest sparks a conflagration. You like that about her, I remind myself. That's why you're friends.

Exuberance has always tugged me forward, pulled me out of the ravine some folks call depression. But it's hard to live with someone you like when she's a straight girl who doesn't notice the electricity between you, even though it's plainly there. Her blinders are so huge and convenient, it's hard not to get snide about it. I walk down the snack food aisle, pulling off the store apron, and set it back in the stockroom.

After work, I don't return to the apartment we share by the ocean. Cramped, with dingy curtains through which a kind of pale, washed-out light trickles. Two bedrooms, though, of course, I'd prefer one. Instead, I ride the F bus away from the coast, through the gray spring downpour—unyielding, sudden, strange—to the next town over, inland, where the hospital is.

The bus is mostly empty and stinks of shoes. Older people, braced on black canes, carrying overstuffed grocery bags and wet umbrellas. A lone, young mother in a ratty sweater, no umbrella, with her infant in a hot-pink rain jacket. The rubber on the floor of the bus is puddling. The driver taps the brakes, taps them again. We lurch forward and back with empty expressions. It's hard to see anything through the smear of wet on the glass, the swishing windshield wipers, their rhythm like a heart beating too fast. I glance at my wristwatch. I'm not quite late yet, but close.

When the bus stops at the hospital, I jump off, shouting my thanks. I sprint through the lobby and take the elevator to the third floor. Up to the clinic where they're conducting the pain study. The pain study is the fourth medical study I've done in three years for money. I'm not going to ask or take money from my parents like Violet does. Her dad's a rich investment banker, or anyway, upper middle class, if you think there's a difference. Mine are schoolteachers. Violet keeps telling me I need to get a different job, and maybe I should deal Ecstasy on the side like she does, but I can't find another job, and I can't get caught dealing Ecstasy, I just can't. It's a white coastal town—people hire people that remind them of themselves, and that's not me, it's never been me—I don't say this because Violet is beautiful and I am not, but because I get the feeling it might wound her to be reminded how sharply different our situations are.

That's not true! They didn't mean it like that, she'd say when we were in high school and then community college together and I'd point out how racist someone was. Is it because he's white? What if I made comments about brown people?

I don't say it, but the thing is, she does make comments when she's not thinking carefully about me. How I might feel about what she said. Once I think this thought, though, I immediately feel guilty, like I'm betraying her, betraying our years of friendship, even though I haven't said or done anything to reveal my thoughts. Thought betrayal—that's not a thing, is it?

I sit down in the white vinyl chair, and Lucy, the research assistant, asks me how my week was. Fine, I answer.

She always wants to make small talk and keep us in harmony for the hour. I try to pretend I do too.

Ok, now how does that feel, scale of one to ten? she asks as she presses the iron against my skin.

Pain floods my skin, sinks deep into my flesh, but not as badly as it could. And there's a flicker of pleasure, which I like, kind of. I'm alive, I'm someone who's out there feeling things. And that's gold.

It's maybe a seven?

She lifts the iron away. I know I'm supposed to provide a definitive answer. Who can tell what your pain is besides you? But I default to asking because it seems, in that moment, looking into her amber eyes, she might know more than I know about my pain. Seriously, she might. My whole life people have been telling me how much this or that should hurt, what should matter.

I'll write down six, she says, nodding in that brusque, secretarial way and scribbling notes on her pad. With a gloved hand, she applies capsaicin cream on the reddish rectangle of skin where she pressed the iron down. I wince at the coldness of her applying the cream, clinical, detached. After so many burn appointments, she knows all the details of my life.

We talk about how my roommate still hasn't figured out I like her. You should tell her, Lucy says in that casual, breezy way, as if she's been there, as if she knows anything about it. Think about it, wouldn't you want to know?

She presses the iron down again. And what's this?

Six? I ask.

Six? she asks back.

I nod. She writes it down on her little pad.

A few minutes later, my phone beeps. An orange alert: our whole town is being evacuated because of a tsunami threat. We've received many of these alerts over the last few years. Ever since a small-wave tsunami a few years ago, scientists have kept close watch on the serene coast that our apartment overlooks, but the threats have all been phantoms. Years ago, all the birds flew away from our town. The opossums and raccoons abandoned us. The drought has meant acquiring our food from the greenhouse farms. Violet skips fresh food altogether, saying it's too expensive, and buys astronaut food online, occasionally lifts from the grocery. We all know why the planet's off-kilter: nobody cares, yet they pretend to care by issuing these meaningless warnings. Violet and I have evacuated our apartment so many times, taking the car all the way up to Portland where her dad lives now, we joke we're just not going to leave next time, come what may. We'll sit and watch for the tsunami that doesn't happen, a blank in our town's history, each day trickling on as before.

Lucy hands me my check. There's one more follow-up, but it's months from now. I call Violet after I leave the pain clinic. A good thing about working at that store is that the owner's never there, so most of the time we can talk on the phone or text bitchy comments about the customers, as appropriate.

Did you get the alert? No bonfire, I guess, I say.

I got the alert, but it's never a thing, right? I mean, am I wrong? It's never a thing, so we should have a bonfire.

Nobody's going to come.

We'll be there. Why isn't that good enough?

It is good enough, I say. Being alone with Violet—it's good enough for me. It's she who expects us always to be striving toward a better scene, a better moment. And the word, the word tsunami. It's a word that freaks me out, a word with so much ominous nesting within it. Yet, after all those other times, how likely is it that this time is different? It's just a word.

I ride the bus back to our apartment, tired employees flooding onto it as we travel through town. The bus grows crowded, and the black rubber on the floor turns nearly swampy from waterlogged shoes, odors of decay wafting through the close air. When it pulls up to the sidewalk at my stop and I struggle to jump off the bus in time, the bus driver almost closes the door on me. It's stopped raining: the sky is a hazy pale blue, and clouds gather and knit, cotton being woven overhead.

Up in the apartment, nobody's inside. The air is all TV dinner, a lasagna with meat sauce or something, and the microwave door is ajar. I wriggle out of my boots and set my backpack down. The living room is in shambles, books lying askew on the puke-beige carpet. The window is open and wet papers are scattered about, no doubt the result of rainy wind blowing in for hours. I shut the window, and the floor is damp on my bare feet. A scrawled handwritten note is taped to my bedroom door at the back of the apartment. *Closed up way early. Gone down the stairs, meet me at the beach.*

I sigh. Of course, she didn't wait for me. She's probably already out there. I look in the refrigerator. Still a six-pack of beer. I grab it, along with jerky and goldfish crackers pilfered from the grocery store. I find a sweater and run down the stairs. Outside, the sky is already dimming, reflecting a dreamy, luminous blue in the pools of water that streak the shadowy sandbar. A dark figure walks along the waves, probably Violet. Otherwise, the beach is empty. The streets are empty too. Not even one passing car. In spite of a fierce gale, I manage to light a cigarette. It's another flight of concrete steps down to the beach, and I nearly tumble down them trying to hold on to the six-pack, the cold metal railing, and the burning cigarette.

The sand's cold, light going fast. The dark figure wandering the edge of the turbulent ocean heads toward me, skirting the reflections of sky in the puddling places where the tide's lapped up sand, and it's not Violet. It's a middle-aged white man with long, stringy hair wearing a trench coat and carrying a bottle. He might be one of the fog catchers. Hey, can I bum a cigarette?

I glance around. Trapped. There's nobody. Just empty sand. For miles. The ocean is endless waves at the shore. The staircase behind me, far away, small. Reluctantly, I set down the beer and start to unzip my backpack.

In a flash, the man has my backpack. He takes off down the beach, his stringy hair streaked with brown flying behind him in the wind. For a moment, I stand stunned, motionless. But my check was in that backpack. I take off after him. He's muscular and fast for someone older, and I'm quickly out of breath. A few paces behind, I reach out, swinging the box of beer bottles, meaning to slow him down with a swift cuff to the back, but there is a smashing sound—bottles breaking—and he shouts, Stupid girl! He makes a sudden left toward a second set of stairs. I trip on a rock and fall onto the wet sand, packed and hard. Rough sand across my lips, dribbled into my mouth. I spit it out. The box of beer smacked the ground several feet away, a few bottles exploding on impact, beer leaks from them slowly. I crouch, dust sand off my body. The light sand abrades the dark skin over my legs, a kind of stippled effect.

Far away, the man bounds up the last few concrete steps. He turns to stare back at me. We look at each other, both desolate, alone in all this vastness. He holds up my backpack, salutes me, and disappears. I needed that check. I feel like throwing up. Why can we never control pain? Why are we always controlled by absence? It's nearly incomprehensible, this ever-present, incinerating desire for what's not there—in this case, the check that represents everything but the slip of paper that it is, the absence of love, the heat of pain on my arm, the sense that my life might have been more than this relentless fear but now will never be.

The sun slips. I've spotted the rare loon on occasion this side of the shore, but instead, there's only the curious emptiness. I empty the broken glass from the beer box, and trudge back with three remaining bottles to the spot where Violet and I usually meet. Up on the road: no cars. Everyone else took the tsunami warning seriously. Violet's at our spot, sitting on a rock in her heavy black sweater, hair whipping around her head, and trying to light a small mound of driftwood with a lighter. I watch her from a distance as she gets a small blaze going despite the wind. She looks up and sees me.

I brought marshmallows, she shouts as I approach.

Where were you twenty minutes ago? I just got robbed.

No shit? She picks up a stick, spears a marshmallow, and hands it to me, a white puff, giving against the sharp stick.

I explain about the man, using the bottle opener on the keys in my pocket to open two bottles, and hand her a beer.

So we have no food? She takes a long sip of beer, drinks it like it's quenching.

Also, I have no check, I say.

I'm angry at her for her nonchalance. For not arriving earlier—like why couldn't she have figured out I was in trouble?

We should be more connected. We've been best friends for years; shouldn't she be able to predict me by now? If you know some- one, you should be able to read the little signs, you should be paying attention. I knew she would steal marshmallows from the store when she closed up, and that's why I only brought beer and jerky and crackers. I've spent years expecting her to under- stand me. Why do I remain essentially unknowable—is it me or is it her? I try not to let my thoughts show on my face, knowing the rage is irrational. And a turnoff.

I'm sorry, she says sympathetically. Are you hurt? Were the burns bad today?

I can feel tears sliding down my cheeks before I recognize how sad I am: as with so much that is painful, my body expresses sorrow before I do. The burns are controlled, perpetrated against just one part of my arm, a part of my arm that, while I am being burned, I forget, as if it is not my arm but someone else's arm, and I feel it by mistake. The burning is not all-encompassing; it does not hurt as much as being alone. She reaches out a hand to my face. I'm sorry, she says. I don't touch her, but I can smell her, ChapStick and some kind of musky perfume.

I lean forward and kiss her, and to my surprise, she sticks her tongue in my mouth. She tastes like the gluttonous ecstasy and sweet too-muchness of marshmallows, the sour of beer, her lips almost waxy. I put my hands on her hips, her red pleather pants soft beneath my fingers. We kiss like this for a long time, growing cold in the salt-stained wind, the roar of the ocean so loud I can't even hear her breathe. The feel of her lips. This is the only still place. When we pull away, the ocean seems closer than it did. I squint at it. Yes, definitely closer. The waves are bigger.

Maybe the tsunami warning was right? I ask her, tentative, wanting her to say no so we can stay here kissing, wanting her to say yes so we can run. Unsure what I want, the fear flooding every cell in my body.

Probably. She shrugs and gets up. She starts dancing with her beer by the embers. The bag of marshmallows on the sand by the rock where she sat. She beckons me. I stand and look out at the sun setting, shielding my eyes a little against the supernatural brightness. Next to us, the pools of water in the places where the tide spirited away the sand have incandesced into orange, and white, and red striations. Not far enough in the distance, I spy a wave.

Look, I tell her. I point at it. Let's go.

My heart seems to lurch up in my throat, but I can't move, every limb frozen in place. She grabs my hand and squeezes.

The wave is colossal, an enormous aqua-blue wall, almost translucent at its upper limit, so terribly tall and cresting, almost solid, so you can't really see the dimming sky through its green heart. If it ever reaches us, it will crush us, drown us in an instant. Violet keeps dancing, a strange, drunken, floating dance, reminiscent of what she did when we used to sneak into clubs. It's not a dance to attract anyone, and she's doing it even though she can see, clear as I can, death is coming for us, coming in that wall of water blocking out the sunset.

Don't be scared, she says.

I'm terrified. Is this it? The wave approaches closer than ever. Monstrous. The sky's shifted. A dark, turbulent gray, no glimmer on the wave where minutes ago I saw the crest sparkle. There's only sound. Only salt. Raging against the light. No time to go anywhere. Maybe there never was. Everything trickles on as before, until it doesn't. I won't leave her.

STEAM TUNNELS

I N THE DARK, THIS TOWN comes alive with hot steam. We lift the heavy grates and drop into the steam tunnels in the dead of night, under a cool blanket of thin smog and stars. We are hungry, we are tired. We've settled for the danger of the steam tunnels, never having found love. We are ready to leave this earth, and yet by all accounts, we are still on it. We'd sat cross-legged on Telegraph all day, as we had for years, and by twilight, our caps were brimming with loose change and dollar bills. We'd stood at the back doors of restaurants and bars to receive alms from softhearted wait-staff. Many—enough—had obliged. Lately, we've stolen fruit from the farmers market.

None of us have been in the tunnels before, though we've heard about them for years. We have every reason to seek their refuge. There has been talk of removing all of us on the streets from the city. Snatches of conversation tell us something dark and deadly is sweeping the country, but we cannot make out what. We are hiding from the police. We are hiding from our parents who were abusive and controlling and neglectful and cruel, who never thought we were enough as we were. We are hiding from ourselves, perhaps most of all.

As we search for open grates on campus, we hear the loud hiss of the sprinklers, the students flirting, the surge of steam coming from underground. We stop by every grate and try to lift each one, but we make it all the way past the libraries to the Life Sciences building without encountering an open grate. The campanile is chiming midnight when the four of us drop into the tunnels: Leah and Vedica and Maryam and Jane.

Leah is the tallest and the youngest, but the softest in her demeanor, the one most prone to stooping to make sure she doesn't threaten you. Notwithstanding her apple cheeks, she knows how to say no in a way that makes all of us quake with fear, and she's come by that tone honestly. She'd hitchhiked all the way from Nevada to the left coast because her stepfather was a pervert and her mother, a doormat.

Vedica is small and compact and furious. She'd run away from her traditional, conservative Telugu parents, who lived in Orange County somewhere, but wouldn't get into any details of why she left. Filial duty still runs deep, a river of obligation inside her. She shows us, her chosen family, the same loyalty. She is the best of us at talking to strangers, at convincing them to drop their change. She wouldn't frighten anyone, it's true, but she can talk you out of the clothes on your back, and that counts for something when we're together.

Maryam is a ukulele player, uncomfortable with asking for money unless she's busking. Like it's okay to get money for a heartfelt song, but not for just sitting there. She's never said why she left home, but maybe it had to do with music. She might be the oldest of us—her age is a mystery too. We can see the lines, deep grooves, etched under her haunted eyes.

Jane is a tatted-up redhead wearing a leather jacket that's too bulky for her narrow frame, and we suspect she grew up the wealthiest because she doesn't know how to manage the money we get when it's her turn, and she's angry as a mother-fucker on some days but twice as sweet on most, as if she's used to getting her way and shocked when she doesn't.

One by one, we jump through the grating, the first of us, Jane, hitting a stray stepladder someone left behind. It clatters to the ground, and we land on concrete at the bottom. We wipe ourselves off, our asses already wet and dusty from the puddles. There are a few puddles, the residual sprinkle of rain, or perhaps the condensation of steam meeting the outside air, in that small swirl of light directly under. We have flashlights in our knapsacks and we turn them on each other like weapons, laughing. Beams of light rove around the space, in zigzags.

Should we really do this? Maryam asks, waving the flashlight at the tunnel ahead, her face a cipher of shadows.

Eh, they're clearing people out, Vedica says. We can stay down here a couple days. Only a matter of time until they find us. Her face is utterly dark, so the only thing you can see are the whites of her eyes, which have been sad the entire time we've known her, and the occasional sharp flash of her teeth.

Leah says nothing. Sometimes this means she disapproves but isn't willing to say so.

Jane says, Let's go, you guys, don't be a bunch of fucking pussies. Do I have to take charge of everything? And shame, the sound of chastisement in Jane's voice, the unspoken *again*, the stride of her combat boots just ahead of us, propels us forward.

We advance deep into the tunnel, farther and farther, not wanting to lose each other, not wanting to hold hands. At first, the only sound is the sodden rubber soles of our shoes barely scuffling against the damp concrete. Sad, pathetic, lovelorn. We four. But in all that suffocating darkness comes the soft, gentle plucking of the ukulele, Maryam unable to stop playing. She doesn't need light to play, the playing flows without effort, instinctively, like the chirping of a bird. All the old songs, the songs of nostalgia and sorrow and loneliness, flood the tunnels, keeping us company, like a fifth person. We keep going, hardly knowing where we're headed, and when we remember to look back in the dank, thick air, we can't see where the grate is: there's no light, no float of dust motes beneath starlight, no sparkle of light against puddling concrete, nothing to illuminate any sort of path to follow back up into the land of the living.

You're always saying shit like that, Vedica says to Jane belatedly, unexpectedly. Her voice breaks through the steam, like she's walking more purposefully, like she knows where she's going.

Shit like what?

How you do everything. When we all do stuff to contribute. Even Maryam.

Jane snorts.

Why are you picking on me? Maryam asks. The slow calm in her voice, the heat of the steam on our faces are more disturbing than open anger.

I'm sick of it, just so fucking sick of it. She thinks she's better than us, Vedica says.

You know the legend they used to tell me when I first moved out here? Leah says.

What?

A young philosophy professor dragged a student down here fifty years ago and murdered her. She'd confided in her best friend, the guy this professor was mentoring, over drinks earlier in the evening. Told the best friend that they were meeting by the Life Sciences building, the professor was in love with her. There were love letters. Handwritten ones. All signed with an initial, never a name, of course. The guy reported it to the police after she went missing. The professor disappeared. They found her body. It was all cut up. Little cuts, a lifetime of cuts, papercuts and gashes, made in a few hours. She was raped and left to die. They combed these tunnels searching for the professor. Some policemen got chemical burns wandering through here. They looked so hard. They kept thinking they saw someone up ahead in the clouds of smoke, but they never caught him.

Fuck, Jane whispers.

And now, there's probably a monster down here.

But why wouldn't he leave the tunnels? Fifty years? Wouldn't he push up one of the grates and get out? Vedica asks.

Leah's voice is exasperated. I mean. If you want to be all logical about it. Fuck.

The deeper into the tunnel we travel the worse it smells. The steam floods the passageways, and under our flashlights we can see the whitish billows, the thick clouds of steam stretching before us, almost a white wall of it. The stench is terrible, sewage or dirty water offset by a chemical odor. A metallic hum—a light top note in all that steam—but we follow the tunnel, take turns leading, lighting the way with our flashlights. Eventually each of our flashlights loses power. In the stagnant air, everywhere, converges the forbidding smell of things incinerating.

Finally, we spot a cone of light, probably beneath a grate, and move toward it, together, still a single breathing thing exhaling in the steam. Our cheeks are hot and wet. Our clothes are thick and wet, sopping with wet heat, a heat that seems to mean something, since we can't shake it. All the mysterious things we never did aboveground seem to be in these vast puffs of steam, their billows in the dark.

Hey, how long do you think we've been down here? Vedica asks.

Couple of hours, maybe? We grope around in the dark for something to push up the grate. In the corners of the passageways are leaves, fragments of litter, but no stick. Far away down the tunnel, there's a break in the steam. Maryam screams first, but she doesn't move. Her screams fill the space, like some kind of banshee. Toward us through the white, limps a figure, straggling, dark, tattered. We stare, frozen. He stops moving, as if he's contemplating what to do.

Run! Jane says in a loud whisper. We grab each other's hands this time, instinctively, none of us wanting to be first or last—the first might feel guilt at escaping, and the last might be killed, and we do not want to change, we have our dynamic down. We take off down the tunnel back in the direction from which we came, holding fast to each other's sweaty fingers. We're an organism, moving together, navigating the way, our hearts pounding, not sure whose heart we hear pounding. We glance back, and the figure is following us, in his half limp. We think it's a man, an old man, though we can't see the details of his face in the dark. He's wizened but light on his feet, chasing us with the springy vitality of a younger man. He doesn't make any sound, and we run as fast as we can, we keep running through the tunnels. Perhaps he doesn't want to catch us but simply wants to make us afraid, and so he follows as we backtrack toward the grate where we entered.

Up there, Maryam says, pointing at a streak of light. That's got to lead up to ground level. It looks like where we came from.

We head toward the light. We set the stepladder upright, and Jane climbs up and kicks the grate so hard, the momentum throws her backward, and she falls onto the concrete. Vedica climbs up and feels along the edges of the grate, like she's hoping she can somehow peel it open, as if it's a soda can tab.

The figure has caught up to us but stays standing in the white, steam bathing him, watching us try to move the grate, as if he knows we'll fail and he's got all the time in the world.

What do you want? Vedica asks. He doesn't answer and she repeats the question.

He just stands there, looking at us. After a few moments, he moves forward.

Run, Jane says, grabbing for our hands, and we run. We run for what seems like infinity, but is probably a few hours, fleeing through the tunnels, searching for a ray of light that might signal a grate. We might remember these tunnels, but every tunnel is just like every other tunnel, so any memory is meaningless. Every time we think we've reached a place we recognize, we realize we don't know it at all, even if it's like the last place. Like is not the same, but the likeness makes us think we should respond the same way. There is the heat, there is the sweat on our necks, the dampness of our clothes clinging to our skin. None of our flashlights work anymore. They've been out of batteries for a long time. Nothing but the sound of clicking, all of us clicking our flashlights.

There, Vedica says. And we see it ahead, lamplight probably. Lemon-tinted, broken into squares, bounded by shadows as it filters through the grate, a glimpse of the future, in which we escape all this darkness.

Is it the grate we came out of? Vedica asks.

Who cares? We just need to get out of these fucking tunnels, Leah says.

We charge ahead, the figure pursuing us, somehow spry when he wants to be. Perhaps he is holding back just for the pleasure of holding back, knowing he has the advantage, knowing the tunnels that we don't. He grabs one of us, we don't know who, her wet fingers slipping away from us into an everlasting night. We spin around.

He's dragging her into the darkness. Maryam and her ukulele. He's dragging her with what we assume is an arm clenched
around her neck, pulling her backward through the dark. She's
soundless, maybe he's got her neck clenched too tightly, his
force against her windpipe. We hear nothing. At first it feels
inevitable. When he pauses, it's astonishing, like he could have
taken us any of those times, but only now, when we're worn
out, panting, exhausted, does he take advantage of this moment to steal Maryam from us. And only Leah has the fight
left to run at him and Maryam, but the figure keeps moving.

We chase this figure as hard as we can, but when we speed
up, he speeds up. He anticipates us. How many has he handled
this way?

One by one we stop, throats raw and burning, our eyes
tearing up, hunched over in the dark, panting, unable to keep
fighting what feels inescapable. We collapse on the floor, no
longer holding hands, breathing too hard and fast to note it as
breathing. It's more a persistent, long rasp, a struggling for life.
The figure keeps lurching forward, more slowly now that we've
stopped running.

Maryam disappears without a sound. It's just us, sobbing
in the dark. Our only family is each other, and now one of us
is gone.

Time passes, too much time to feel, and slowly our breathing
quiets, reconciled.

Should we try to find a way out again? Vedica asks, tentatively.

We can't just sit here, crying, can we? Leah jumps up. She's
been knocked down more than any of us. And so, we follow
suit. And we feel less certain, as we hobble through the tunnels, looking over our shoulders, wondering what might lie
behind us.

We walk, and we walk, and we walk. It feels like we walk only a few minutes. It feels like we walk years. Underground, we can only estimate time by how tired we are. When we see that lemon-tinted spectral light again, we move toward it as one. We are trying to open the grate when we hear the figure approaching. We sense him before we see him. And he's upon us again. But this time when Jane kicks the grate with the force of terror, we are at her back, holding her up. She pushes through first. Leah kneels on the ground, letting Vedica step on her shoulders so she can help push Jane. But before we can pull Vedica up, she falls and steps on Leah's hand. Leah cries out as Vedica rises out of the steam tunnel. We throw one end of a sweater down to Leah and raise her, just as the figure reaches into the light. His hands are old, crepe-paper hands, bleached oh so pale from lack of light.

Get me out, get me out, Leah is screaming as we pull her all the way through into the light by the Life Sciences building. Through the enormous glass wall of the building, we see the enormous dinosaur bones inside, a resurrection. We look at each other, the halo of white light surrounding each of our heads, the light radiating off our hair.

What happened to you?

I don't know.

What happened to you?

Our clothes are in tatters, our skin caked in grime, our hair white. We look at each other, aghast, uncertain. We are full of questions, and those questions weigh on our hearts. We cover the hole with the grate we pushed aside and begin walking. Though the dinosaur is still standing, the campus is different. The air is syrupy and hot. The grass is old and brown and faded. The sun is coming up, a pale white disk slowly rising. There are no people, only buildings. We pause at the place where we entered the steam tunnels.

Should we stop at the gym and try to sneak into the showers? Jane asks.

We make our way to the gym. We don't pass a single person, and when we try the door, it opens easily. Inside it is pitch-black. We take hold of each other's hands and pass through the eerie quietness to the empty shower stalls. They're perfectly dry. We feel around in the dark, running our fingers over the tile to find the faucets. We turn each one. They don't work.

After we leave the silent gym, we reach Telegraph Avenue, where there is no one, just one long, empty gray street stretching before us. We walk toward Oakland, looking at each other every once in a while, too frightened to speak.

Our bones are tired, cracking. We breathe heavily. The sunlight casts three long shadows. One missing. We walk and we walk, all the storefronts flooded with sunlight, things deteriorating in that light, the stores empty of people, as if a plague has wiped out the people of the city we loved. We walk for miles, trying to get our bearings, and then one of us whispers, so soft we could choose to miss it, but we don't.

Did time pass us by?

Is it past our time? Yes.

HOW WE KNOW OUR TIME TRAVELERS

HE STRIDES INTO MY ART studio with a vitality and energy you can't fake—the métier of the young. No paunch, no white hair at the temples, no slump in his shoulders, no half-hearted efforts at a flirtation he already knows is marked for failure. All the artists in the neighborhood have flung open the doors to their homes, their sheds, their cramped makeshift studios, their lush gardens, and people meander into these spaces to look at art. Often, they pretend they're going to buy something—to be polite—but most of the time, they're simply seeking the pleasure of looking, of taking something with their eyes they don't have to pay for or give back.

Standing before one of my installations: a young man, nodding. Not only young, but gorgeous. Jet-black hair, eyes shielded by sunglasses, each lens an iridescent swirl of oil rainbow, skin darkened like summer velvet. He's the spitting image of my husband, down to the constellation of black moles on his neck—but thirty years younger. His arms are sleeved in a sky-blue sweater. My heart catches, a strange kind of ecstasy, and I immediately want to introduce myself, to slowly, carefully, roll up the sleeves of his sweater, to run the tips of my fingers along their warm surface and find his familiar tattoos. He might be my husband, my family. Not just a simulacrum, but the real thing, the human I've lost somewhere in the present.

My husband has decided not to come, as per usual, and has fled to the gallery he owns in the city. He hasn't visited any of the artists participating in Open Studios in years. He's lost interest in art, he says, even though it puts food on our table. What's the point? Nobody's genuinely moved by it. People are faking it, people are desperate to seem sophisticated, he says, as he drinks himself into an absinthe-flavored stupor; there's no reason to hold back, as there are several more bottles of absinthe in the garage, a thank-you gift from a celebrated artist who sculpts phalluses in varying postures and places waxed mustaches on them.

My husband's in a midlife crisis, but unwilling to admit it, even as all the rituals of crisis come into play. He likes to fill the bird feeder in the backyard lemon tree and watch the hummingbirds flap around it, their elusive wings holograms. He likes to take his time eating, chewing every bite of his cereal slowly, methodically, feeling the easy give of grains under milk. He goes on long, uphill rambles, drifting into the fields with his hands in his pockets, for the sole purpose of looking at the goats far up in a field facing the city to see whether any have died. He's interested only in the minutiae of mortality, and it's taken a grievous toll on our marriage, which has been constructed on an edifice of art, on the edifice of art as a real agent of change in our world. Our relationship's built not on art, but on a shiftless artifice, I realize now.

It's scorching. Artists offer Dixie cups of lemonade or wine, and most people choose wine no matter how thirsty they are, or perhaps because of how thirsty they are. Milling around my husband's double are people of every persuasion:

in hoodies, in T-shirts, in designer business suits, in leather pants, wearing hoop earrings and red lipstick, waists cinched in corsets, flowy gauze skirts, piercings like shooting stars all over their bodies. They enter the shed in our backyard, following gold balloons and pasteboard-and-marker signs. Back in the day, my husband would have enjoyed people-watching, if nothing else.

I wanted to blow off this yearly ritual, too, close my doors. I'm too far along in my career to care much about opening my studio to the public. Long ago, I thought something life-changing might occur at an open studio, that a stranger might walk in and change my life, and the anticipation of the unknown fueled me through the small talk, made me ever more aggressively entertaining. Now I know nothing changes merely because you let people look at your work; everything is the same afterward, at least for you. It doesn't matter that you're hoping your work moves strangers, changes them in some way they cannot immediately articulate. My paintings have grown tame, tame enough to sell, tame enough for living rooms in the heartland even, but I never managed to beckon fame or a legacy, and I understand now, I never will. Yet, force of habit compels me to participate in this pointless ritual, even if I need to do it alone.

Before throwing open the shed doors around noon, I'd guzzled espresso and painted for hours. I'd stretched two linen canvases and primed them, covering my fingers and hands and overalls with gesso. I'd swirled alizarin crimson into ultramarine. I'd flung blue oil paint onto a canvas entitled *Moon, Womb* I'd painted last week, the image of a titanium white and quinacridone magenta moon with the shadow of an embryo cast against it. My husband's double is ignoring the paintings, as he should since they're shit. He gazes at an older installation I've left on the wall as a kind of litmus test for how easily a viewer succumbs to shock: a wall of unwrapped tampons, hot-glued together, each string casting a skinny shadow, the wall meant to show how the body's most visceral needs, its deepest reality, serves as a barricade against all else. Next to the tampon installation, from the same period: a wall of birth control dispensers, each painted in streaks of carmine and purple lake, luminous seed pearls nestled inside, in place of pills. My husband loved these installations once upon a time, but now he thinks they're garish and vulgar. Too needy and erotic and attention-seeking to say anything meaningful, he's said.

I study my husband's double from across the room. I want to find out if, in fact, my husband has traveled across time to find me, perhaps to tell me something important I should know about our marriage, perhaps to reveal what I don't already know about the past that led me to this lonely, barren moment, perhaps to warn me about the future. What if he's found a way to break the space and time between us? I would know it was him if the double has the same voice as my husband. I just need him to speak. How else would we know our time travelers if we run into them, except by the way they appear, except by the way they move around a room. We might be the only ones to recognize them, the only ones to understand that time has been breached.

My husband was once beautiful, and here he is in this young man. Perhaps the sunglasses are an affectation, a way to cloak intense vulnerability—they had been with my husband when I met him. I imagine sliding the sunglasses to his brows, slowly, gazing into the seductive brown eyes I already know, carefully removing the sunglasses from his face, running my hands along his cheekbones.

But he won't look at me. He's resolutely closed off, even after he abandons the wall of tampons, and walks around, peering at the paintings with his hands stuffed in his corduroy pockets and an impenetrable air, occasionally nodding or grunting at the art, whether in affirmation or unspoken criticism, I can't say.

Other visitors swarm around him, but he stays laser-focused, like he's truly come to view art, and not necessarily for the free wine and Brie and crackers, nor to mingle with others or pick someone up. I breathe in deeply and cross my arms, almost to protect myself from this younger version of my husband, from the sense of lost, slant magic that floods me as I gaze at his countenance. Can I help you?

He glances at me and pauses. You the artist? he asks, as if he already knows the answer.

It's my husband's voice. Same intonations, same elegant accent, same eliding of the *r*.

Yes. I nod uncertainly.

When I was browsing online, yours was the studio I most wanted to see, he says. He holds out his hand, and I shake it with some reluctance. So, he doesn't recognize me, except as the artist.

Your work! It's phenomenal. I love what you're doing with even the most mundane objects, the most mundane experiences. Menstruation. Birth control. I love it.

He keeps holding my hand. If he isn't my husband, he should have released my hand immediately. And there's the pleasant nature, too, of his grip. The peculiar way his hand is precisely the right temperature, no sweatiness, no clamminess, the feeling of it against mine—like we have known each other, intimately, for years. I don't want to let go either. The room full of strangers spins around us, and I think again of rolling up his sleeves, taking off his sunglasses, but he releases me, and I suck in air.

You okay? he asks.

You remind me of someone, I say. And when he looks at me with an utterly blank face, I want to shake him. How could he not know? It's maddening. It must be a hoax. I wrack my brain to consider who might be trying to play this joke on me. Who have I pissed off?—I shuffle through names.

He does take off his sunglasses and puts them in his pocket. Who? he asks.

Helter-skelter flecks of bronze in his eyes, identical to my husband's, but there is no recognition in them. I scrutinize his jaw, his cheekbones, maybe too closely, hoping, I don't know for what. Silence consumes us both. He looks at me like he thinks I'm flirting with him, and maybe I am, because I am, in my own mind at least, flirting with someone I've known for thirty years.

He touches my cheek. Electricity—startling, overwhelming, painful—passes through my skin, conducted through the water in my body, reverberating like waves in a pond after a stone's been skipped.

You have some kind of, I don't know, orangish streak there. Were you painting this morning?

I nod. He takes his hand away.

Can I see the work?

As soon as he asks me to see the work, the sound switches back on, and I understand we aren't alone, we're surrounded here in this room with many other people, all of whom I'm supposed to be courting. I've inched toward him in my effort to properly see his face and am now standing far too close to him: our faces are inches from each other. His pores are identical to my husband's, but I'm not sure whether pores can be different. I don't know if it's he who's closer to me or I to him, or perhaps it's just natural, when we're standing in the midst of so much noise and commotion, but close like this, I observe the crooked bump on the bridge of his nose, and the way his upper lip curls ever so slightly with contempt. I know that contempt, the contempt of the young.

I take him to see the new canvases, which I've left leaning up against the shed outside to fully dry. He paces in front of them, cagey.

They're ... different, he says finally, stopping in front of an encaustic I experimented with. Different than what you've got hanging inside. Your embryo fixation is interesting.

Fixation? I ask, tension in my shoulders. I've been hoping he'll say he likes these, that he understands what I'm going for, that he understands me. This is what I want most of all—the way I'm always hoping my husband will understand me, even though he never has, and probably this guy, his double, never will either.

Maybe that's too strong a word? Fascination? Isn't that a kind of hat—no that's a fascinator.

He smiles a little, quizzically, like he's not sure what he's done wrong, but knows that there must be something.

My eyes might give me away. He steps back, hesitation animating him, and begins edging away. It's all I can do not to grab him by the arms and pull him back toward me as if we were still in college at a party. We met, drunk off our asses, in the co-ops at Cal. He'd liked my art, and because he'd liked my art so much, he'd invited me to eat cheese flautas like the ones his abuela used to make, and drink icy margaritas, and this was how we'd ended up in bed together that sultry midsummer night, and why we'd moved into an apartment off campus together the following year. Never again had it been the way it was that first year, the first year when we fell in love. Or the first year we married, trying to halt our inexorable slide away from each other. We didn't know then that marriage is a way to be sure you never know someone as he is when he's alone, not entirely.

Do you have children? he asks. His eyebrows draw together, making a tent squiggle in the center of his forehead.

No, I can't.

I regret immediately saying too much, even though he asked. Embryo fixation. I can't tell if it's the embarrassment about my own artistic obsessions or a need for this young man to know me intimately, the same way that I feel that I know him because of his resemblance to my husband. But I'm always saying too much, letting spill details about my life, like I can't bear to keep anything to myself, like I need the comfort of other people knowing what's inside my mind, like I need to express myself at the cost of social order—and that's, I've found, a high cost to pay. What does my fertility have to do with him? Nothing, nothing, of course, nothing.

I'm so sorry, he says, aghast, and steps away, and again I want to pull him closer.

It's okay. I'm past that stage of life.

I say it flatly, no emotion. Sometimes it still hits me with a painful force. Children will never happen for me, not if my life continues the way it's been going. Not if my body keeps aging against my will.

My wife and I are thinking of having kids, he says, his voice calm anew. I glance at his finger. Sure enough, a plain platinum band circles it, the same band my husband has.

You look like my husband, I say in a broken voice. Last-ditch effort because my longing has become unbearable, a kind of excruciating stretching and breaking inside, remembering the person I was when my husband and I first met—how much I long to be that person again instead of this other person, less accomplished for her age but with more silver hairs, and yet somehow hungrier, ravenous, despite being older.

He looks at me more closely, without alarm now, his eyes wandering my face. He's noticing me. I hadn't realized he wasn't before, and it's only the contrast between before and now that makes me understand that I've mistaken interest in my work for interest in myself. Maybe, in fact, he's here only because of my canvases, and not to sweep me back in time, after all.

What other studios are you planning to visit today? I ask politely, a last face-saving question. Disappointment and humiliation have assumed control of my body, rendered it merely a blushing host, triggering in me helplessness, hopelessness, fragility. Visitors are beginning to leave the studio, slipping out one by one, and two by two, and I should get back inside, I should play hostess.

He shrugs and glances down, embarrassed. I was interested in your work, in the materiality of your brushstrokes. No other artists in the catalog caught my attention. When are you finished here?

My eyes meet his. The bronze flecks. My husband liked my brushstrokes, too, their juicy thickness, he said. I glance at my watch. I'll be closing up in about a half hour, I say.

Do you need to get back inside? He looks like he wants me to say no.

So, it's not just me. There's something hanging in the air between us, a curtain to be drawn away. I say I do.

I'm going to grab something to eat for lunch, he says, but I can come back. He pauses before asking, Want something?

No, that's okay, I say. The trays of cheese and water crackers might still hold enough after everyone leaves.

He touches my forearm, lingers there a moment. Electricity, the jolt of that, him and me sharing the same space. But the moment passes, and he walks away, and he doesn't look back.

I hurry back inside and mingle with the stragglers. Answer questions about what medium various works are in, how long it took me to install those tampons on the wall, how long it took to install the birth control dispensers, what glue I used. They don't ask much about meaning, about how my life informs the work. They aren't interested in the meaning, I realize for the first time in my career. It's all about how it makes them feel. My intentions are irrelevant to the art's reception, and maybe my husband is right to take such intense interest in the hummingbirds, in the speed of their metallic wings, in their zealous emptying of the bird feeder. The crows invading our neighborhood. Maybe that's all there is in this life.

The last visitors leak out of the studio, having bought nothing. My work, which had seemed so vital, so charged in the morning, is leached now of all excitement, of all the blood and sweat with which I'd made it. Merely paint on cloth. Nothing.

I throw empty wine bottles in the recycling, sweep up crumbs. The Brie and crackers are gone, though voluptuous curls of cheese remain on the edges of white plastic knives, and I regret not taking the young man up on his offer of food. I adjust paintings on the wall, a number of them askew. Plainly, people were touching them when I was outside.

You use impasto, I remind myself: you want people to want to touch them. The desire to be touched is embedded in the paintings, their raised surfaces, the work done rather violently with a palette knife so that you can feel, looking at the rough surface of the paintings, life pushing at the edges, life in the pthalo blue swirled with cadmium yellow, in the naphthol scarlet glazed with transparent orange. These paintings are meant to be consumed, taken in with gusto and digested, rather than simply seen, passively, from a distance, with a coldness.

This is how my husband sits on the redwood bench in our backyard, entirely still, watching nectar vanish from the feeder. Not in warm absorption. It's in a kind of quiet alienation, estrangement.

I left the studio to chase a dead end, yet some visitors felt what I wanted them to feel: touch me, touch me. I glance at my watch. He's not coming back. I should go get something to eat. I go outside to fetch the new canvases and bring them back inside to be varnished.

My marriage, the vacuum of silence it is, all the things unsaid gathering weight, pressing down on us over the breakfast table. I wonder if this younger version of my husband is here to talk, openly, the way we used to talk, like true confidants, rather than with the muted politeness of strangers. All that talk eventually leading us to understand there is no real knowing of each other possible, no amount of talk to bridge the gap between us, between how we see art—or how we see reality. How I wanted to stand revealed within my art, how I wanted to be loved, and how, after years of toil in the art world, years of crackers and cheese, he came to understand art was of no more importance than boxes of cereal. All the glamour mere illusion, all the right people saying all the right things. We had invented each other at the start, only to unmake each other over the years.

An hour later, as I'm drinking the dregs of a bottle of wine, there is a knock at the door. My husband's double. He hands me a brown paper bag. I thought you might have changed your mind, he says, and smiles, his eyes crinkling in the corners.

The foil-wrapped package is still warm to the touch. Underneath the foil, flautas that look like they're from Mario's on Telegraph Avenue. That Mexican joint's been closed for years and years. I look up at him. Do you want to sit down?

We sit together at the table at the front of the studio. I hack the flauta in half with a white plastic knife. Warm cheese oozes out of its crisp golden shell, a pale white pool on the black plastic plate. I pick up a half and take a bite. It tastes real. Are you . . . ?

Yes, he says.

Is he lying? Entirely possible. I want so deeply to believe he's my husband, that he's come to carry me away from my present to return to the past, to start over, to live life over, but better. Now that he's simply admitting he's my husband, like it's no big deal, I realize, with an ache in my ribs, he might not be. I am old, old enough now to be his mother.

I see the differences between him and my husband, little differences, like how his eyebrows are just a smidge narrower, his lashes slightly longer, thicker, and yet I reach over. Tiny differences don't shield me against the desire to be with him, to be with my husband as he once was. There are ways time makes us; there are also ways it fails to shelter us, ways it fails to offer a buffer against the way we've been with each other. Slowly, I roll up the sleeves of his knit blue sweater, hoping to see on his arms those indelible marks of past and future.

ASSEMBLY LINE

ASHLIN COULDN'T REMEMBER QUITE HOW she'd arrived at this job. In fact, she couldn't remember ever teaching another enameling class, or even what she'd done before she started teaching. She knew quite a lot about enameling and jewelry, but the source of her knowledge was a mystery. When she reached into the recesses of her memory for her first experience of enameling, the day when she fell in love with it, she pushed up against darkness and clouds. There was yesterday, and perhaps the day before that, nothing deeper.

While her students were working on their necklaces and bracelets and abstractions, she came around to each of the large, pale, scarred worktables, offering encouragement and tips. They seemed to know her well. A white teenager in skinny jeans joked around and wanted to know how the cloisonné necklace she was making at home was coming along. An older brown lady asked her to demonstrate sgraffito as she'd promised last week, and even though Ashlin couldn't quite remember the promise, she used a bamboo skewer to scratch into wet enamel. In the back corner of the room, she paused in front of Jason. He was long and gaunt and angular, all elbows and knees, with graying black hair and deep-set eyes. Hunched over on his stool, he was using a paintbrush to transfer wet red enamel onto a circular copper pendant. His intense, meticulous focus reminded her of someone.

How beautiful. And who is this for?

He shrugged. Oh, I don't know. My mother, maybe?

For a few minutes, they talked about how to use the dry sifter to cover more ground with flat color. She showed him how to gently tap the sifter to control a transparent silver shower of enamel particles through the mesh. Now you do it, she said. He used it expertly, but looked up at her, as if to see whether she approved. It was endearing.

His lower lip twitched as she talked about the possibilities of firing the plate repeatedly. Images of layered enamel shuffled through her mind as she spoke. Describing the mystery evoked by one transparent layer of color over another and another, she felt as if she were summoning her words from an encyclopedia.

You okay? she asked.

It sounds complicated, maybe a little outside my comfort zone.

But you're doing a fantastic job for someone enameling for the first time. I like how smoothly you've layered the color. I'd never guess you were a beginner. What do you do for a living? Ashlin knew this was a question people asked each other.

He paused before answering. I guess you could say I'm in artificial intelligence. So, anyway, I think this is done and ready to be fired.

Oh, a tech guy! There are so many of you, aren't there?

She carefully carried the pendant to the nearest kiln and put it in for two minutes at 1450 degrees.

She glanced up at the clock on the wall. She hadn't gotten the hang of time yet; class was already over, but it felt like it had just begun.

Okay, everybody, looks like it's just about four o'clock. Time to clean up your stations. Leave any unfinished work on the trivets and bring them over here for safekeeping. We'll fire them next week.

Ashlin pulled Jason's pendant out of the kiln and left it to cool on the front table with other student work, all of the reds, blues, greens, golds gleaming in a pool of sunlight. The students cleaned their tables, returning the vials of enamel powder and tools to the storage cabinets. Thank you, some of them called as they drifted out.

She went to Jason's worktable. He was the kind of only neutrally good-looking man you might easily pass over, nice but subtle cheekbones, square chin, reflective eyes like water or glass, no fire in them. And yet she felt pulled, dreamy, magnetized to his side by an unseen force.

Would you like to get a coffee with me? he asked, pulling an olive messenger bag over his shoulder.

His smile seemed open, friendly. But there was a dark intensity in the way he looked at her, a cryptic expression she couldn't quite read, and the mystery held her back a little, made her wonder if there was something sinister in the invitation. I would like that, she said finally.

All right, let's go. I know a quaint little coffee shop nearby. We can walk there.

They strolled down the concrete breezeway of the community college, and then into the cold spring. A sweet current of magnolias and star jasmine eddied through the smell of hot dogs from a food truck. Mallards, escaped from who knew where, splashed in the puddles formed by the bumpy gravel of the driveway. Walking with Jason, the world seemed new. He took her by the hand and led her through the oleander, through a split in the chain-link fence, and for a moment, she was reminded of fairy tales and wondered if this was a magic portal, but on the other side was a parking lot of the strip mall where the coffee shop was located and a garbage dumpster.

You like caramel macchiatos with almond milk, don't you? Jason asked when they approached the counter.

Ashlin considered. I suppose so, she said. How did you know?

I had a feeling. He ordered an Americano for himself.

Anything to eat? he asked.

She shook her head.

They took a round table in the corner of the empty coffee shop and sat stiffly there, clutching their drinks as if they were fortification. Where did you go to art school? he asked. It seemed an innocuous question, but it took Ashlin a moment to retrieve an answer. The conversation continued that way, a series of his assured, confident questions and her halting answers. He seemed genuinely interested, and his questions were good, when she thought about them, and because she couldn't figure out what troubled her about him, she leaned into the stumbling conversation. She tried to get a handle on it, tried not to make a fool of herself.

She looked at her watch. Again, time trickling away, two hours had passed without permission.

I should get going. She stood.

So soon? he asked.

I have to make dinner.

I'd love to take you out to get something to eat instead. He reached out and touched her arm.

Ashlin nodded reluctantly. She felt dizzy, in thrall to him. She wasn't even hungry.

They ambled to the Chinese food restaurant on the other side of the strip mall, dark and full of high-backed, carved rosewood chairs with plastic covers on faintly iridescent seats.

I used to come here with my girlfriend all the time, Jason said, leaning forward and speaking in an intimate tone. We'd sit at this very table. She was vegetarian and ordered the stir-fried eggplant with basil.

Oh, that's what I was looking at on the menu, she said.

I always ordered the Kung Pao chicken.

Perhaps she had known this already.

He ordered for them, and they talked about his relationship with his ex-girlfriend over beer. How he'd fallen in love with her at first sight, and they'd moved in together within a month, spending long Sundays in bed daydreaming out loud about all the places they would travel together, and ordering takeout. They'd lived in a crappy little apartment with peeling paint and creaky floorboards. Its wide windows faced a wall with a brick façade and no sunlight ever entered.

After a while, I came to see that wall as a metaphor, he said. We were going nowhere but that apartment. We are still stuck in that apartment as far as I can tell, even though I've long since bought my own house.

As time passed, the girlfriend had become distant and secretive, or so Jason claimed. After a long list of complaints, he concluded with a regretful sigh. Three years after we began, she announced she was going to India to visit her grandparents and might not come back to the States. She'd decided there was no place for her here, or with me.

Where in India? Ashlin asked. A creeping sensation arose at the back of her neck and crawled, spider-light, between her shoulder blades.

Madurai.

That's where my parents are from. She shivered, though she had no recollection of her parents or her childhood, only facts, just as she couldn't remember her experience at the school where she'd learned to make jewelry, knew only rote answers to his questions about it.

Hers too, he said. She was a Tamil Christian.

Same.

His face disclosed no surprise.

AFTER DINNER, ASHLIN RETURNED alone to her studio apartment on a nondescript, leafy street. It was spare, mostly unfurnished, carpeted in an ugly, thick beige with stains, perhaps made by an errant dog. A pull-out futon in one corner. In the other, her desk, covered in pliers, copper wire, a soldering iron, drills, paintbrushes, a plastic palette, and jars of enameling powder, and trivets. Everything looked untouched, some items still encased in plastic. No signs of the cloisonné project her teenage student had mentioned. She turned on the light for the concrete balcony. Facing a brick façade, it held a small bright-blue electric kiln that looked new. She went outside and opened the door of the kiln. No drips, no dark streaks, no evidence of prior use. Next to it, lay oven mitts stiff in their newness and dark glasses.

She couldn't remember why she'd chosen this shitty apartment when she so strongly preferred beauty, a jewelry maker by trade. Perhaps it was all she could afford? She returned inside, and as she poked around the apartment, she considered the hours with Jason, not sure what to make of them. They'd accumulated without any sense that time was passing. Nothing in her body bound her to the hours, not hunger, not desire, not loneliness. She sank onto the couch, struggling to get past the feeling that she'd stepped into an elaborate diorama and searching for a sign that she'd chosen all of this, the way she'd chosen to get coffee with Jason. She felt something cool pass across the round of her stomach and back, a phantom touch. What was that? The sureness of the touch, a cold palm. It was as if her body and its peculiar sensations were not her own. She shivered.

The sensation passed and Ashlin moved to her worktable and began peeling plastic off the seals of little jars of enamel. She cracked them open, feeling self-conscious, as if whatever had caressed her stomach were there in the apartment with her, an incorporeal presence observing. She drilled a tiny hole into a rectangular scrap of silver sheet where she could hook the necklace's clasp. Using a utility knife, she cut a tiny stencil of a man in a sheet of plastic. After placing the stencil over a small round silver plate, she began sifting golden opalescent particles over the man. They rained down. Golden shadow man. Who knew what it meant. She removed the plastic stencil and kept looking at him, wondering.

Jason called Ashlin the next day and the next, he called her every day until enameling class came around the following Saturday. Sooner or later, every conversation returned like clockwork to his ex-girlfriend. At first, Ashlin was discomfited. He was clearly still in love with this ex-girlfriend, so why did he keep asking her out? It was perverse, his obsessive need to keep unspooling these stories of a young man and woman who'd been young and stupid and in a kind of fiery, jealous, all-consuming first love. He recounted their conversations, including her accusations in their last exchange that he was a fetishist. But you're just attracted to who you're attracted to, he exclaimed indignantly, as if Ashlin had made the accusation too.

In class, she tried to make sure she didn't favor him over any of the other students, not wanting to rouse suspicions. She wondered if the others could tell: she felt her cheeks flushing every time she went by his desk, feeling his gaze on her body. After class, they went for coffee again, and then dinner at the Chinese restaurant. He invited her to his place, but she demurred, saying that she was his teacher and it wouldn't be appropriate until class ended.

In spite of the many phone conversations, the revealing of intimate details, she felt no closer to him. He unsettled her. He acted, at all times, as if they knew each other much better than they did. Weeks passed this way, he inviting, she declining. Alone in her apartment, she would feel the phantom caress and would try to rub away the sensation, but sometimes it would come back.

At the start of a new month, she trudged downstairs to the super with check in hand, but he said rent had already been paid through the year. A chill passed through her. Queasiness. Her stomach flooded with dread, and yet she smiled, tight-lipped at the super. As she rode the elevator upstairs, she tore up the check. Inside her apartment, filled with uncertainty, she wondered if the walls had eyes, if anyone could see her inside these four cramped walls, this shoebox, if there was anyone she could call in case of an emergency. There was nobody, only the fear.

On the last day of class, when Jason invited her to his house, she nodded. It was better than nothing, the odd thread of familiarity that bound them, the only connection she could remember having. From the front, his house was not especially grand, though they entered under a portico, but it was located downtown, where real estate was expensive, and inside, it was more spacious than she'd anticipated, full of rooms and long, winding corridors. She wondered how he'd known of her little community college class, why he'd traveled to that other dilapidated part of town when he lived here and, based on the unmistakable opulence of the interior, the burnished steel and granite and classic hardwood, he could certainly afford more lavish classes.

In the kitchen, Ashlin ran her hand along the cool kitchen countertop as he cooked pasta puttanesca. He gave her a taste of the sauce on a wooden spoon, making some comment about capers and red pepper flakes, and so she smiled with appreciation, even though she'd noticed recently, with a mild curiosity, that food, however prepared, bored her, even as it excited others. She was never hungry, and yet others took such relish in consuming it, licking their lips, eyes sparkling, that she longed to feel that way too.

He left the dining room light off and they ate in silence by candlelight. His long nose and thick eyelashes cast fine shadows across his hollow cheeks. She remembered how open his face had been on the first day; it seemed the closer they grew, the more he receded into himself. How long ago did you and your ex-girlfriend date again? she asked casually.

Oh, I don't know, fifteen years ago maybe?

And you haven't dated anyone else since? She tried to keep the judgment out of her voice and ate an olive out of the puttanesca.

I've never asked you about your ex-boyfriends, he said, defensive.

I can't remember them at all, though I feel like I have some, must have some, she said truthfully. He didn't seem surprised.

She slept over that night in his giant master bedroom. He operated the lights and blinds by remote; the touch of a button and all went dark. Between the satin sheets of the bed, he touched her with profound familiarity, expertly moving her along the knife's edge of desire, as if they'd fucked many times. It was disconcerting, his hand on her stomach for a moment before moving on. His grace distracted her from the moment.

She'd had an idea that sex with a new partner would be something exciting, maybe even revelatory, but when she examined this idea, tried to remember where she'd first heard it, why she thought it, she realized she couldn't remember any exciting first time. When she plumbed her memory further, she couldn't remember having sex with anyone else at all. She hit a wall where a memory might be.

Soon Ashlin was staying over every night. Jason had taken an early retirement from a robotics firm and spent his days in his study working on a project he declined to discuss. She left her spare toothbrush on the side of the slate sink adjoining the bedroom. She examined the insides of his medicine cabinet. A few different pill bottles; she didn't know any of the medications. A toenail clipper, a pack of razor blades, hyaluronic acid serum, a black comb. Nothing menacing. Sometimes while he slept, she wandered the halls, peeking into rooms, trying to figure out why he had so much space, what he did with the enormity.

Do you want to move in? he asked at the end of the month.

She still hadn't seen the whole house, but it was infinitely more comfortable than her tiny apartment and he was the only person she knew, so she shrugged. Why not?

ON THE NIGHT SHE moved in with her suitcase of clothes and boxes of jewelry-making supplies, it was improbably raining, the first days-long break in the latest drought. Sheets of rain hit the side of the house. In the distance, the hills slipped into a murky brown under the gray clouds and would soon turn green.

As she stuffed stacks of folded clothes in the half of the oak dresser he'd allotted her, he said, I don't want you to go into my study under any circumstances. I need total privacy to work, and I don't like anyone going through my things. You understand, don't you?

Ashlin agreed. It was shady, but like him, to set a condition to their cohabitation after she'd given her notice at her apartment building. He explained that his study was the room farthest from the master bedroom. You travel down the hall, into the long corridor, and make a series of turns. Right, right, left. It's the last room. Leave it alone, eh?

Every morning after they ate toast and eggs together, he'd disappear down the hall to work. He'd set up her studio in a front room adjacent to the foyer, and she spent many hours alone there, only leaving the house on Saturdays for the enameling class she still taught. She hung the pendant of the golden shadow man she'd made the night they met from the desk lamp, wondering why she didn't have more jewelry to show for her experience. What had happened before the first day when she met Jason in class?

You don't need to keep working at the community college now that you live here, he would say over the breakfast table. You could just spend your days making jewelry, like you've always wanted.

I don't know, she'd say.

You're not trying to meet someone, not trying to leave me, are you?

Sometimes in the late mornings, when the muse was taking a particularly long time to alight, she explored the house. She avoided the end of the corridor. No to the right, right, left. She'd scrounge around in the boxes that cluttered the spare rooms or the exercise room or the garage, or stroll around the rose garden in the backyard. But one day, she caved into her curiosity: right, right, left. At the darkened door to his study, she listened. She heard nothing. No doubt, the room was soundproof. She returned to her studio and wondered again what he might do in that room all day. Perhaps he was inventing something new and exciting. Perhaps he was trying to raise money to start a new company. One day when he went out to his meeting with investors, she snuck down the corridor and gently tried the knob of the forbidden door. Locked tight.

Though she couldn't be certain how much time had passed, a day came when she found a crate under the bed in one of the spare rooms overflowing with school records, letters, papers, and photographs. Jason's life in a box. She picked through the photographs. Images of sophisticated enameled and soldered jewelry, images she remembered as if from a dream. He'd said he had no experience—he'd lied. Then she remembered him saying that his ex-girlfriend had been an artist and jeweler: the photographs depicted her work. She found a picture of Jason, perilously young, his light eyes flooded with sunlight, taken at some sort of afternoon party. He was laughing. A young woman, almost in profile, wrapped her arm around his stomach, trying to pivot him away from the camera. Her hair was black, curly, a long tangle, precisely like Ashlin's hair. She caught her breath, touching her hair, as if to make sure she still had it. She dropped the photograph back in the box and shoved the crate under the bed, her chest tight with anxiety.

The next week, she followed Jason down the corridor. From around the corner, she heard the loud jangle of keys as he unlocked the door to his study. The heavy door creaked as it opened and shut.

He remained such a mystery. She began to watch him more closely, looking for details. His schedule was consistent. Regular meetings with investors on Mondays, lunch with other entrepreneurs on Fridays. He kept the keys to his study in his pocket, except at night while he slept, at which time he set them on the nightstand, next to his water glass and whatever self-help book he was reading.

She wanted a peek inside his studio. A year of living together had passed and she still didn't quite understand what he did. His secretiveness, the chill between them was almost too much to bear. Although he'd been willing to share intimate details of his past, he rarely ever talked about what he did for work and now his taciturn nature seemed alarming. It's robotics, he would say, shrugging. You're not interested in that. You won't understand all the technical stuff anyway.

Once she'd started paying attention, she could discern sounds coming from his study. The sound of grinding machinery. Foreboding engulfed her heart at their candlelight dinners.

One night, Ashlin set her phone to vibrate at midnight. She woke with a start at the thrumming in the pocket of the robe she'd worn to bed. Jason slept through the light sound, still in the argent moonlight filtering through the casement windows. She thought he might awaken at the whining of the bed when she rose, but he didn't move in the slightest. She slipped over to his nightstand and picked up the keys, clutching them tight to keep them from making a sound. The house was so silent, she could hear the whisper-soft *shush shush* of her cotton socks rubbing the floorboards.

The corridor was pitch-dark, but for a square of moonlight coming through the skylight. On the other side, it turned pitch-dark again in the final turn. She fumbled with the keys, worried that the sound of metal on metal would echo from the high ceilings, reverberate to the bed where Jason slept. Perspiration pooled under her arms, slid down her cheeks.

The creak of the door. Inside, the dark room was cavernous, cold and fresh like winter. Her fingers fumbled over the smooth lacquered wall for the light switch and flicked it on. The light was bright and fluorescent. She blinked as her eyes adjusted.

When her eyes adjusted, it was a line of life-size automatons lying on iron racks she looked down on, naked, their feet facing her, eyes shut. Brown skin, curly black hair, rosebud lips. Each her spitting image. They were perfectly motionless, vulnerable, as if sound asleep. She thought she could see the barely perceptible rise and fall of their breasts, or was that what she wanted to see? Her skin crawled, the insides of her nose prickling with the smell of solder and metal and heat, and yet she moved closer, scarcely breathing. Who are you? she whispered, less to the dolls than to herself. For it occurred to her, they were not merely very similar to herself, but pure duplicates. Their existence meant her own was endangered. How many versions of herself could there be?

And sure enough, when Ashlin gently touched one of the automatons on its soft, spindly brown arm, she felt a ghostly, tender touch on the skin of her own, and goose bumps broke out over her body. When she stroked the soft tangle of her hair, she felt the hairs on her own scalp shift. A frisson of excitement and fear exploded up her spine as she touched her small, cool ear. Her heart clenching, she ran a hand slowly across the automaton's stomach, and a warm phantom hand caressed her own stomach, and moving down, left a strange feeling between her legs as it had so often when she lived in her apartment. She jumped back as if the automaton had struck her.

Its eyes remained closed, a taunt.

A few yards beyond them, at the other end of the room, rested an enormous stainless-steel box: a machine twice the size of any one automaton. Its large circular door opened out onto a conveyor belt that carried the automatons to the horizontal rack. She slipped alongside the wall through the narrow space between the edge of the rack, where one of the automaton's hands hung off the edge. As she moved slowly toward the machine to examine it, she glanced back over her shoulder to make sure the automatons weren't waking up, feeling certain they were, that they were coming up behind her. Next to the machine, a wide desk held a large computer with an office swivel chair before it, probably where Jason worked. Covered in papers. Taped to the computer monitor, a small photograph. Nubby edges, that classic tint of Kodachrome. She recognized herself in it. A serene, mountainous place where she'd never been, the sea an impossible blue behind her. Skin crawling, she touched her smiling face, trying to remember. Who had she been? And when? A prickly dread coursed through her. The violent nausea of seeing herself placed on her back, as if asleep, each robot lying next to one another, fingers touching. Recognition dawned on her. They could be her, but more terrifyingly, she was them. They'd glided along in her place. Or perhaps they were about to be exchanged for her.

Ashlin ran her hands around the sides of the machine and found a silver button that appeared to be an on-switch. She pressed it tentatively. The machine jolted to life. A loud whirring like the metallic flutter of an enormous dragonfly's wings reverberated. She looked back at the line of automatons now tinted blue by the light flickering above the circular door. The roar of the machine filled the room.

So you found them. Jason stood in his pajamas at the door, blinking at the strong light.

What is this? she asked, although she already knew.

They're you, he said. Or you're them. You're all duplicates of my ex-girlfriend Ashlin.

She shivered at the sound of her own name.

I always thought she'd come back from India, that we'd get together one last time, but she never did. Mutual friends from college told me she died in an accident there. Years passed. I couldn't forget her. I kept thinking about that old apartment, that brick wall, how she'd left me behind. I began working on reconstructing her, on reconstructing you, using old photographs, everything I knew about her. I didn't know everything, of course, but I coded you all the best I could.

Do they . . . feel anything? She gestured at her duplicates, feeling herself bound irrevocably to them, and to her name-sake, evidently the only version of herself that was real.

No, you're the only one that's conscious for now.

Then what are these for?

They are my spare Ashlins. You're all connected. But you can only program so much memory into automatons.

What does that mean? She thought she knew, but she wanted to hear him say the words.

You play around with consciousness, you can't know when one might rebel. The last Ashlin did.

He leered at her and ran a palm down the arm of the au-tomaton closest to him. She felt his hand stroking her own arm. The other arm was her arm. The nameless dread that had been floating through her for months coalesced as he lowered himself on top of the automaton, and cupping her breasts for leverage, slid inside Ashlin.

THE NEXT MORNING, SHE woke in his bed, and went out to the breakfast table where he sat reading the news on his phone. Wordlessly, he made her toast with marmalade and scrambled eggs and coffee. She looked idly through the picture window as she ate, and he returned to his phone. Outside, the sky teemed with enormous storm clouds. A neighbor rambled by with her pug. Two men jogged past, talking loudly about the stock mar-ket. Ashlin longed to leave. But where would she go? He might not have programmed her to survive other situations. Perhaps he'd simply bring in another who would sit here at the table eating toast with marmalade and scrambled eggs, daydream-ing about nothing, before disappearing into her studio to paint particles of glass onto copper plates. For all she knew, she was already not herself, and last night when the automaton had been abandoned on its rack, and she and Jason had finished on the floor, he'd lifted her sleeping body onto the rack and replaced her with one of the other Ashlins. Memory was elusive, but she could recall other selves. The flash of them laid out on an iron rack. The warmth of a phantom hand on her stomach, of him inside her, a feeling that she would remember, for who knew how long. But all the days and nights before the last had begun to blur together, a mysterious abyss of time—how had she met Jason again, had she always been here in this big house?

She touched her neck and felt a necklace circling it. She lifted the pendant. A scrap of metal, a gold shadow of a man on silver. Pretty, mysterious. Why was she wearing it? She picked up the newspaper and began reading. Wildfires. Fascism. A pandemic.

Anything exciting happening out in the world today? he asked with unnerving calm. Not a question so much as a threat, and she smiled to calm him.

Oh, you know, it's the world. Same old.

THE GLITCH

1

LATE ONE AUTUMN EVENING, THE holograms stop obeying. You're sitting at your computer, at the kneehole desk in the study, fixing lines of code, grief lodged inside you, still after all these years, a feral thing. Your wife's hologram is a bluish phantasm, nearly transparent, yet like enough to the real thing. Just as she did when she was alive, she sits cross-legged on the couch, reading the newspaper, gasping at headlines.

From a pipe installed in the rafters, jasmine wafts in, her scent. Quixote curls at her feet, shimmering blue, licking his paws, unable to stop. Your son and daughter skate through the house at top speed, sliding down banisters. They never travel without roller skates anymore. They shriek with recorded delight, never aging. Once in a while, they shout, Can't catch me! You smile to hear it.

Black smoke from a faraway wildfire obscures the moon. Can we live through any more of these fucking headlines? your wife asks. You glance at the clock. Her programming is off. Right about now, she's supposed to say, Should we order out for dinner?

To your surprise, Quixote stops licking his paws and barks at the open window, which is something he did quite often when he was alive, but which you didn't program into his hologram. From the open window: crowds that were camped out in makeshift settlements are moving down a hill away from the blaze. A shadow across the yard. Probably nothing. Surely the creek will stop the flames.

You shut the window. Quixote stops barking, returns to the floor by your wife. He keeps looking up at you and whining. He's waiting and panting. Not in his code.

You check the program, and it's a jumble with strange, intricate changes to the code. You didn't make them. The system. It may have been hacked.

2

ANY WAY TO FIX this mess? You stare at the monitor, trying to find the problematic bits, but there are too many of them, stacked on top of each other, their import muddled by each other. Your head's about to explode. Rewrite the code—calm down, calm down.

Code should be streamlined, and yet you find yourself adding duplicate exclusions: Your wife cannot swear. Your dog cannot bark.

Your son skates into the room. I'm bored of skating, Mommy, he whines. He's not supposed to say that. He should never get bored. Boredom is for the ungrateful. Your daughter crashes into him with a short, frustrated laugh, knocking him down. They look up at you from the floor, their eyes big and round.

We're booooooored! they say. Can we go outside?

Your heart catches in dread and anxiety. A familiar question, this, a question with which you were frustrated during their lives. The holograms were programmed to be happy. The holograms should not need their own special entertainment. They are off script.

They skate around the study, arms outstretched, knocking things off shelves, full of hilarity. Your wife turns the page of the newspaper and looks up, a blue scowl on her lips. Can you take them outside? I need to know what's happening to our country, she says. Off book again.

You breathe deep, striving to maintain your calm.

The holograms can't leave, they exist only within this house. You've constructed what lies within these walls with such glorious precision. Your wife continues scowling.

There's only one thing to do. You put your hands on the children's backs and lead them through the foyer to the front door. You throw it open. Stars above the foothills. Stench of smoke. People migrating across the hills. The world's burning. It's terrifying.

Happy now? you ask.

3

YOUR CHILDREN GAZE OUT the front door, entranced by the smoke and stars and faraway fire. Sound floats into the house from the darkness: songs of abandon, songs of sorrow. It's the slow strum of ukuleles and guitars made by the people moving across the dark foothills, a background music of clinks of glass. Singing their way through darkness.

Where are they going? your daughter asks, gesturing at the mass of shadows. Her code shouldn't have allowed her to ask the question. Her voice is that of somebody older than she was when she passed away.

Your son says, They're looking for a home, dummy.

Don't say "dummy." Their houses probably burned down— they're searching for shelter, you say.

Your wife emerges, carrying the newspaper rolled up in one hand, as if she's about to use it as a weapon. You taking them out to play or not?

We can't go outside, you say. Look at what it's like out there. No rain for months, air thick with burning grass and oak trees.

The children look at each other and laugh. With delicate coordination and trepidation, they step across the threshold of the front door in their skates. They should come to the door and find they can't pass through it. But nothing stops them, and somehow they don't vanish without their laser source. They slowly, quietly, roll away.

Skating past your car parked at the top of the hill, they glance back at you from the top of the long, steep driveway and smile.

They skate forward, first stunned by their new abilities, then cracked open in anticipation. With a shriek of glee—like they are at the top of a roller coaster—they begin their descent down the driveway and soon slip out of view.

Are you going after them? Your wife advances upon you with the newspaper.

You flee into the night.

4

NIGHT AIR SLAPS YOUR face. Gravity pulls you down the drive-way. Your lungs burn as you chase the children. Tough to breathe. An acrid taste fills your mouth. Your eyes sting.

You can't catch them in time. Where driveway empties into street, unable to keep their balance, they collapse in a silver-blue heap, their transparent limbs pretzeled together under the glow of the streetlight. Their shrieking turns into wailing. High-pitched weeping. Pain and humiliation. Defeat.

Is it possible the holograms have hurt themselves? After your children's deaths in the wildfire, you coded them to perform love and joy, never pain. All these years, it has been comforting to know the holograms aren't suffering, not suffering the way your corporeal children had suffered. The way the rest of the world is suffering.

It takes a few minutes. By the time you arrive, they're disentangling from the heap of them, still sobbing loudly. The soles of your bare feet are raw, abraded, bleeding. When you reach for them, your hand turns blue as it passes through them. Right, right—simply projections.

Someone rolls out of the shadows, hovers next to them. A bald man in colorful rags riding a unicycle, knapsack and guitar case strapped to his back. As he balances, a light clinking from what sounds like bottles knocking together comes from inside his knapsack. Know where the coder lives? he asks.

His voice is smooth and pleasant. You're the coder, but you're vulnerable here under the streetlight. The world, so dangerous, is so full of clashing needs and desires and not enough of anything to satisfy them. Could you take this unicyclist? Maybe.

5

NOPE. NO CODERS HERE, you say. The dissonant music comes closer.

The stranger wobbles to and fro, precarious. He telegraphs skepticism with his eyebrows.

That your house?

Who wants to know?

He frowns. So that's how we're playing this? You program all these wildfires and refuse responsibility?

Can I learn how to ride that? Your son points at the unicycle.

There's a whole group of us rolling down the hillside. We can show you. The unicyclist whistles long and low, jerks his thumb.

In a moment, you and the children are surrounded by a jamboree of strangers on unicycles. Dressed in rags all colors of the rainbow. Some play instruments as they ride. Guitarists, flautists, drummers. Notes from an oboe emerge, a thread of melancholy in the wild din.

She the coder? a man with tiny brown braids shouts, jerking his finger at me.

The bald unicyclist nods. Those are her kids.

A sunburnt, more clean-cut woman rolls into the center of the circle as the crowd of vagrants whirls around you. She dismounts and straightens her knapsack, and there is the distinct sound of bottles hitting other bottles inside the pack as she offers your son her unicycle. Your son removes his skates. They lie blue on the ground. She holds the unicycle steady. Her kindness makes you want to cry.

Another man cycles over, offers your daughter his unicycle. Steadies it for her.

The children topple, remount, balance.

The woman looks defeated. You coded all those wildfires, and now you won't even take responsibility?

I didn't code any wildfires, you say. I have nothing to do with the way the world is now. I didn't do anything. Pressure builds inside your chest. You can't even get your hologram children to obey you. Why is this fucker blaming you?

Didn't you? the bald unicyclist asks. Weren't you a contractor for the government? He shakes his head with disgust.

And then you wonder if he's right, if you might just be responsible for this mayhem.

6

THE BALD UNICYCLIST JOINS the other unicyclists encircling you. Faster, faster they ride, blurring together beneath the light from the streetlight. Their tunes shift, increasingly jangly and off-key. The glory, the destruction. The night sky reddening from the fires. You want to shout stop. Stop. You also don't want to show how fearful you are.

Who knows who these people are. Why have they come? The stress, the chaos, the sounds are overwhelming. You retreat into yourself, the one quiet place, sinking to the asphalt on your hands and knees. Beyond the whirling rapturous circle of unicyclists, the interminably long driveway. How do you reach the house, how do you get to your computer to fix the code, to save the world? Your house is so inconsequential, so far away under the stars.

Yellow lamplight glows through each of the windows. Your wife is tiny beneath the porch light. She grips the newspaper like it's an Uzi. She's managed to cross the threshold of the front door, notwithstanding the code, but she doesn't descend. You wave at her, hoping she interprets it as a cry for help. She waves the newspaper cheerfully in response.

And just as grief threatens to overwhelm you, split you open here on the asphalt, the bald unicyclist whistles, jerks his thumb. One by one, unspooling, the unicyclists slowly ride out of the circle and into the street with the man and woman who donated their unicycles to your children riding piggyback, rags streaming behind them. You watch your children roll away.

Wait! I admit it. I am the coder. It's me. It's my fault.

Your son turns and waves. The whole shimmering blue line of unicyclists escape down the dark hill, taking your children with them.

You weep as you shamble up the driveway toward the house. The children were projections, but they were *your* projections.

7

YOUR WIFE HAS DISAPPEARED inside by the time you open the front door. Panting, Quixote runs to greet you. I could've used you outside, boy, you murmur. You wonder whether your children's code will change again, whether it will one day tell them to return home. Probably not.

You trudge down the hall. In the study, your wife stands by the window, holding open tomorrow's newspaper. How can she stand to examine the horror? Astonishing, the fortitude with which she's programmed. She had carried one child, and you the other, but you remember her pregnancy, and her labor, too, as being sturdier somehow, and you'd been envious then, but it brings you joy to see the trait resurface now. Quixote paces.

You hope to catch a glimpse through the window of the unicyclists traveling down the foothills, glowing blue, some glimpse of your children. Instead, it's the blaze approaching, much closer than it was before the unicyclists appeared.

Paper says there's no containing those wildfires, your wife announces, matter-of-fact.

The first wildfire. In which you'd lost your family—their bodies. You'd forgotten to say goodbyes, returned to a burnt shell of a home. Fire trucks and ambulances and smoldering ashes. You rebuilt your house. It was insufficient, so you rebuilt the whole fucking world, its foothills, its trees, its streets, as far as the eye could see. Holograms to stand in for your beloveds, to say their lines, to console you. For hours you were at your keyboard until the world was serene perfection, not a wildfire in sight. But, of course, it was a starry-eyed plan. Nothing you code could keep danger at bay, keep loss from your doorstep.

You place a jazz record on the player, you won't go gently. Quixote circles you, barking. Your wife whirls in a pool of light. She tries to press against you and her blue arms pass through yours in an attempted embrace—a failed embrace. Here, the wildfire will find you.

THE ENCROACHMENT
OF WAKING LIFE

JUST AFTER NOON, I DRIVE over the Golden Gate Bridge. Nuclear fallout from a bomb that detonated more than four hundred miles away and years ago in Seattle left it standing, a shadow of what it once was. Black rust creeps from the edges of its beams into the dulled red paint, like waking life encroaching on a dream. The lunar blue of the water seems higher now, closer to the bridge.

Looking at this new, broken landscape through the car window, I'm too horrified by the changed world to comprehend it. To shake myself free of the pain of those exploding stars—the host of blood-red stars exploding around the plane. After each burst, a second explosion inside my head—a rapid expansion followed by an equally rapid contraction. The pain in my head had been so acute it'd slipped into ecstasy.

Seeing my misery, the fur-hatted older man sitting next to me on the plane had shaken his head. I managed a whispered account of impulsively sneaking onto what appeared to be an outrageously expensive flight from Barcelona to SFO. I'd already rushed through customs and was sitting inside the terminal when my flight home was canceled, I told him. It seemed like a sign, even a minor miracle, to see another flight to SFO about to begin boarding, even if it was an airline I'd never heard of before. I'd managed to slip past the gate agent unseen as he collected tickets. Is this my punishment? I asked Fur Hat, even though he was on his fourth bourbon.

I didn't understand that the flight was flying into the future until Fur Hat explained that I was in the company of members of an exclusive time-traveling club. In the course of repeated investigations, during which scientists had determined that colonizing another planet to live on would be unduly risky, difficult, and expensive, they had also learned that time might seem like an impenetrable barrier to another moment in the many light-years of history, but it was possible for us, as specks of stardust, to slide through it in places, like moving around on a viscous sea current, not once from here to there, but over and over. The past, the present, and the future are a space made of something like sheets of water on top of each other, waves sometimes cutting through different parts of the space at once, he said. And truly the concept those words delineate is outdated, dear, as all moments happen at once, together, coalescing with each one flavoring the other. It takes language so long to catch up. He nibbled on the thin orange peel garnishing his drink, unfazed by its bitterness, and warned me things might be different after we crossed the time barrier; that my presence might confound, even frighten those who'd forgotten me.

Even if Fur Hat had told me about the burnt edges of this future, I wouldn't have listened. I'd thought only of how it would feel to see the boy from whom I'd been separated during a study-abroad program in Barcelona—a boy I was desperate to see, and who I hoped was desperate to see me too. During our time apart, my longing for Rama had been so overwhelming, so laughably big, I often thought I might pass out from it. In all of history, had anyone ever ached so much to see another person?

A few minutes later, I'm standing and sweating in the shade of a gigantic live oak, across the street from a small white Craftsman bungalow. The air smells like ash. Like the bridge, all the edges and corners of the house are blackened. A pandemonium of wild parrots erupts against the white sky. When I raise my hand against the bright light, the length of my palm is inadequate to the task of blocking the sun, which hadn't seemed this close in the past. My chest tightens with anticipation—and sudden worry—as I approach the house. In the driveway, a sedan is parked askew on the concrete, as if someone careened into the driveway too fast and slammed on the brakes. I have to smile—how like Rama, impetuous and rowdy, forever challenging cars to races on the freeway. But driving a sedan, a boring family car. My Rama?

Through the picture window, an older man is playing piano with a young girl. Then he turns his head to the side, and I'm startled to recognize Rama, thicker around the torso, with flecks of silver in his hair. But still Rama, I guess. Aquiline nose. Burnt-umber skin. I move closer to the window and hear the familiar *bum-bum-bum* of the ivories. He and the girl are playing "Heart and Soul."

During our last phone call, on my way to the airport, I'd sensed the distance that had grown between us during my six months in Barcelona. He wasn't missing me the way I was missing him, so much as developing a dangerous kind of indifference. Perhaps it was my recognition of that change, not just my desperate longing to see him, that had prompted me to sneak onto the other airplane after my own flight was cancelled.

You may not be able to go back, Fur Hat had said, looking at my worn clothes.

Hesitating in front of the door, the doorbell right there, before me, I try to ignore the prickle of weird, cold dread within me. I've made it this far. I can't go back now. The piano playing stops. Probably the pizza! someone shouts.

Footsteps, and the door bursts open. A girl clutching a wad of dollar bills. Where's the pizza? She must be his daughter.

Hi. I'm sorry, I don't have it. Is your father here?

Rama limps to the door. He looks at me with dismay, hovering behind the girl. Vaidehi? Vaidehi Varadarajan? I don't believe it.

Believe it, I say, my voice too high.

You look . . . exactly the same. You haven't aged, not even a bit. He shakes his head. I thought you died.

No, no, I'm alive. I smile. I shift from one foot to the other. His face remains impassive. He doesn't invite me inside.

The last of my excitement drains away; all I feel is a leaden disappointment.

You know, I suspected for years your parents were lying to me about your whereabouts. That you'd dumped me without bothering to tell me. You'd ghosted me.

But we're so in—I catch myself. We were so in love. I wouldn't have done that.

He rolls his eyes. Yeah, I guess we were. You remember how I was in those days, a diehard romantic. Too many Bollywood movies. What a fool! I waited for a while. I kept thinking you'd turn up. If you were really dead, they'd find a body.

His daughter scrunches her nose and taps a foot, seemingly in discomfort; it could be strange to think of your parents attached to strangers before you were born, I imagine. Whatever her own origin story is, our love story threatens it.

They didn't find a body because I wasn't dead, I tell him.

I try to reconcile the twenty years of memories he has with what I don't have, but it can't be done. The gulf between our minds, our experiences, is too wide. I wonder if we can cross it, get back to where we were. Hope stirs. If there was a connection then, there could be now, a gravitational pull, years that were too minor, too short set against the eternity of the university, to erase.

This is my daughter, Lucy, he says. My wife's still at work.

Nice to meet you. I hold out my hand, but Lucy eyes it like it's a foul-smelling shoe. Can I come in?

Yeah, I guess so.

Lucy heads upstairs. Rama gestures at a seat across from him on the couch, next to a big orange tabby cat, who hisses at me when I sit. She jumps off the couch and runs out of the room. She's usually so friendly, Rama says.

The couch is mottled and rough like sand, such a prosaic, functional piece of furniture I can't picture the Rama I knew ever picking it out. Along the taupe wall are framed professional photographs, many of them portraits of an aging woman with ice-blonde hair. But there is the encaustic with a large embryo on it. He'd gotten it for me at an open art studio off Euclid Avenue long ago, where we'd been drinking too much of the talented artist's wine and giggling over her tampon installation, and then wanted to commemorate our happiness and make it up to her by buying the encaustic. Afterward, we'd gone downhill for hot links and cokes. I got on the plane to Barcelona a few days later, and he promised to babysit the encaustic for me. He's kept it. My heart rises in my chest.

So how've you been all these years? Rama rubs his ears. A familiar gesture, made strange by his age, and something catches in my throat.

Can I give you a hug? I ask. I've missed you so.

Without waiting for a reply, I reach over. His body stiffens, as if guarding itself against me. His palms remain planted on the couch as I cling to him. After a moment, I release him with an awkward laugh. So, fill me in, what have you been doing? I see you kept that painting.

Rama's nose twitches. He jumps up and begins pacing around the room. He shakes his head, confused. It's as if he's forgotten; as if he's trying to shake off the present and come back to me.

I stayed in Spain for years, I say. Flustered by his silence, determined to fill the awkward silence with something other than tears, I make up a story. I tell him I was knocked out by a robber near the La Sagrada Familia.

And then I lost my memory for a while. That's why I didn't get in touch.

Rama looks around the mantelpiece as if a tchotchke has gone missing. I wonder if he believes me.

So you're married now, I say.

Am I? Rama's nose twitches again.

Yes, your daughter, this house . . . it's all a little overwhelming, you know?

Right. Right. Our house. He eyes the photographs on the walls and shakes his head again. I was waiting, I feel like forever, for you to come back.

How did you meet your wife?

Rama plunks down on the piano bench with a sigh. You didn't call, he says in an accusing tone. We loved each other, but you didn't pick up the phone for twenty years. Was I so easily forgotten?

I promise you, I never once forgot about you.

As he lopes around the room, I sort the memories that flood me. Sunlight dappling Rama's face as he slept in one morning. The lush fragrance of star lilies he bought me on a whim as we passed a flower stand at twilight, and how allergic I'd been to them but didn't want to tell him. Him bustling around the kitchen frying dosai and making coconut chutney, leaving the dishes for me to wash. Spooning one night, when his hand cupped my breast in a weirdly possessive gesture I hadn't liked. None of these particulars had occurred to me while studying in Spain—or if they had, I'd dismissed them. I'd spoken of him to friends not as a person in his own right, but merely as my boyfriend, a deep and affecting absence in my life. I'd believed myself to be completely in love, but now in this moment with the real him, I feel uneasy. All my old doubts about him, thoughts I'd suppressed in Barcelona, come rushing back.

You say you had amnesia. So how did you retrieve your memory? he asks.

I cross my arms. I do not like being cross-examined. He's looking at me like I cheated on him.

Before I can think of what to say, the doorbell rings and Lucy charges down the stairs. She returns to the living room with a giant pizza box. Are you staying for dinner? she asks me.

I look at Rama, who squints at her beneath narrowed eyelids. There's something unnatural about his voice as he asks, What am I doing here?

Dad? Want some? Lucy opens the box and pulls out a slice of vegetarian pizza.

I stand and exhale. It was a mistake to come here. It was lovely to meet you, Lucy.

Vaidehi, you just got here. Rama rubs his temples, a frantic motion as if he has a migraine. Stay!

Have a slice of pizza, Lucy suggests.

No, thanks. I'll get out of your hair. I'm sure your wife will be home any minute.

Pizza sauce dribbles down Lucy's chin. What's wrong, Dad?

Dad, Rama echoes. He looks at Lucy as if he doesn't recognize her. He twitches, his head movements strange and disconcerting, a different creature bobbling underneath his skin.
Why do you keep calling me that?

I've got to get going. I back away until I reach the front door.
Is this new life going to be nothing but a series of fresh sorrows?
A child losing her father as he reclaims his former self, the self
I want. A child experiencing the inverse of what I felt when I
came into the house. Stunning, the emptiness of not quite recognizing everything I've ever known, the familiar stretched beyond recognition in a funhouse mirror. Now she feels that way.
My whole world writ uncanny -but perhaps Rama had been
like this all along. Had I lied to myself about who he was, who
we'd been together? Here in the future, anything is possible.

Take me with you, Rama says in a too-loud voice. We need
to catch up.

I turn to open the door, but he lunges and catches hold
of me. His fingers are digging into my arm, and I start to feel
a little fear, but I also feel excited, like I'm getting away with
something, and I can't quite distinguish the two.

I'm coming with you, he announces.

Dad? Lucy says again, frightened.

What's going on here? Who are you? Rama shouts at her.
His daughter's face. She begins to cry. He releases me and I rub
my arm. He was holding on too tight.

I manage to get through the door, but Rama follows me as
if it's simply expected. My rental car glows, a red lozenge under
the white sun. I lift the ponytail off my neck to wipe off the
sweat. Rama goes to the passenger door and climbs in.

I take my place behind the steering wheel. I'll drive us
around a bit, and then bring him home again. You just terrified your daughter.

Daughter? He shakes his head again, harder. No. Vaidehi, you've been saying some strange things. You all right?

I know something is deeply wrong. My presence, my appearance—not having aged—is deeply confusing, even frightening, to Rama. Fur Hat warned me to be careful. I should put Rama out of the car, send him back inside to his daughter, but I can't bring myself to part from him. Not yet. Just a few hours before, I'd been so desperate to see him, I'd snuck onto a plane just to reach him sooner. Surely there's no harm in talking to him for a little while before I decide where to go, how to make a life here. I've been waiting ten months or twenty years for our reunion, depending on how you look at it—I can't leave without knowing what happens next.

We fly down the hill. I barely brake around the curves. He gazes out the window as if, like me, he's seeing the entirety of the landscape—the eucalyptuses on the bluffs stripped bare of their leaves and heavy with wild parrots, the old, cracked roads, the too-close sun—for the first time. Notwithstanding the gray in his hair, he almost has me convinced he's right in his delusion that he is still his former self, as unfamiliar with this future as I am; no time has passed and we're as much in love as we've ever been.

I think of the white, furry bondage cuffs; the Bollywood movies we watched; the way he used to transport me far from who I'd once been, a little girl in nubby, secondhand Kmart clothes. I feel the old rhythm. All moments happen at once, together, coalescing with each one flavoring the others, Fur Had had told me, and I can almost hear him, the smell of bourbon and the whir of the plane blending with the cheap clothes my mother had gathered while searching for discounted items, holding the dresses and shirts by their white plastic hangers. I am in both places at once.

But what if I rescued Rama from this marriage, this awful future? What if we drove north up the coast, and started a brand-new, lighter life off the grid, growing our vegetables and fruits and lavender and raising goats? Would his marriage travel with us into the future too? Surely not. Surely, we could transcend all of that.

Rama turns on the radio and scans the stations. Whoa. Some of this music is out there. He settles on an oldies station that plays songs from the start of our relationship. Oldies? He snorts. I tell you, songs are getting called 'oldies' quicker and quicker these days.

Rama, these songs *are* old.

You're wrong. This came out last month. He fiddles with his phone for a moment. No signal, but I'll look up the release date later.

Has he always talked over me?

It came out years ago, literally years ago.

We drive around the small tourist town, crisscrossing over the hillside roads with their houses like intricate chromatic blocks and eventually passing the floating houses, arriving at a strip of restaurants on the waterfront, beyond which float every kind of sailboat imaginable. One, I notice, is the *Relentless*. We argue about old music and outdated politics, and it feels as if he's coming back to me, but instead of giving me pleasure, the return to this way of being together makes me nauseous. Was it ever thus? I park downtown so we can walk along the waterfront. When I buy a paper bag of saltwater taffy at a candy shop, Rama admonishes me, It's just expensive junk for tourists.

I *am* a tourist, I say. Stop telling me what to do.

As we stroll by the shimmering waves, Rama says I was always like this; my opinions are not as carefully considered as his.

He's not the person I remember—or did I imagine that person, invent him in my fervor to be with him again? He's a person so ready for applause that I feel simultaneously disgusted and pitying. Are these constant disagreements something new, or did I simply suppress the memory of them? I'd believed he was worth sneaking onto that plane.

My stomach clenches with anxiety. What if I can't sneak onto a return flight?

We return to the car within an hour. Something gives way inside me and I take a deep breath, trying to find the right words to tell him our love is not real, not timeless, as I'd thought. It belongs in a little compartment in the past.

Ahead, in the distance, a man and woman are approaching. Between them is a tiny girl in a peach frock whose hands they hold, and as they walk, they swing her up. Every time, the frilly hem of her dress flies up and she shrieks in delight. Rama stares at the family, the delighted girl. His eyebrows lift in confusion and recognition. He must be remembering his wife and daughter, remembering that he lives here in the future. I breathe a sigh of relief. If he's remembering, it's time to let go.

I'm going to take you home, Rama. Get in.

What are you? He says it with vengeance, like he's about to bite off my head. What exactly are you?

What do you mean?

You're not Vaidehi. You're not, you can't be *real*. You haven't aged. Are you a ghost?

My eyes fill with tears. I'm not sure if it's him or the too-bright sun, low near the horizon. I am real, I say. I shield my eyes with my hand. I'm just as real as you are, anyway.

If that's true, I might not be real either. Rama sticks a finger in his ear again, as if to quell a ringing. The silver strands of his hair flame in the late afternoon sunlight. But I must be real. I can see my shadow. I can pinch myself. I can think of myself thinking. So then, what *are* you?

I open the car door and sit in the driver's seat, slam my door shut. He doesn't get into the passenger seat: he strides from around the other side of the car, coming toward me, head shaking. I feel vaguely afraid, thinking of how hard he held my arm, like he couldn't let me go.

Let me take you home, Rama. I'm sorry I disrupted your life like this. I just wanted to see you so badly. We were so in love.

His eyes roll back in his head. *What. Are. You?* He yanks the door open and grabs my arm, tries to pull me out of the car. I grab the steering wheel and hold tight. His nails dig into the flesh of my arm. I think of how possessive he'd been, how much I'd overlooked certain interactions in order to preserve our fragile long-distance relationship.

His face looms toward mine. I can see his pores, the shattering wildness in his black eyes. Frightened by the doglike snarl on his lips, the sense that I'd never known him, I bite his cheek hard. As my teeth sink into soft flesh, he yelps and reels backward, clutching his face.

I lock the door with the electronic key, and inadvertently thumb the red panic button. The alarm sounds. I can't figure out how to disable it and so it keeps ringing, announcing *emergency-emergency-emergency*, as Rama hunches over, holding his face.

My violent reaction startles and disturbs me. I'd snuck onto that airplane because I'd loved him intensely, hadn't I? Or had I just made an impulsive decision, to gratify my longing? I cannot say for sure. Nothing has been quite what I'd thought. Maybe Rama had always been petty, small, terrifying. Maybe I'd deluded myself into loving him. *No, no,* it had been love. At least limerence. But here in the future, even if there is no seawall against the past, I don't love him at all—and I don't know whether to trust that either.

Rama straightens, and a thin line of blood trickles down his cheek. Panic floods me. He'll try to hurt me again. I terrify him as much as he terrifies me. We do not belong in this time together, our minds twenty years apart.

I start the car. He pounds on the window. Through the glass, his fists are like slabs of meat squished in plastic wrap. So large and fleshy and unfamiliar. The harsh alarm still blaring, I edge forward. Rama clings to the door handle. I accelerate. I drive toward the southbound freeway on-ramp, whispering to the person I thought I knew: *Let go let go let go!*

The velocity forces him to let go. The car lightens as he falls back. An old pop tune is playing, too loudly, and I flick it off. No sound now but the whirring wind, the hum of the engine. Visible from my rearview mirror, Rama teeters dangerously in the space between before and now, tiny and ruined with one hand up—whether waving goodbye or shaking his fist in rage, I cannot be sure.

I wish I'd never come here, never seen Rama like this, but I can't return to the past. I don't know how I'd find a flight home, how I'd pay for it or sneak onboard again. More than that, I can't imagine returning to the past and waiting, waiting for a future I know is coming. I can't imagine returning to such unbearable knowledge: the boyfriend I love will turn out not to be who I thought he was; a bomb will devastate the West Coast; the world as I know it is going to end—and I will wind up like this again, alone. Always alone. I don't know where to go, how I can go on. But perhaps that was true before, too, and it's only now, here, that I'm recognizing it. There was always going to be this long drive on a highway stretching away from the timeless shifting waters of the bay toward the misty hills, toward a mysterious, unknowable future and the world in all its unfeeling destruction and dark glory.

THE MOMENT

WHEN I LEAVE THE APARTMENT for a date that afternoon, Ma's chopping eggplant in the kitchen to make kathirik-kai poriyal. Bold knife strokes, no fear she'll nick herself, where if it were me, I'd have already sliced right through a finger. Since Pops left her and moved to Morongo Valley several exits away, she's been doing better, cooking more, running her seamstress business, watching her reality television programs, but sometimes when I come home from work, she's just sitting on the couch in the silent dark, with the window open, and it freaks me out a little. Okay, so it's not happiness she feels, but it's *better*, is what I remind myself. If Pops were still here, he'd already be watching the football game, and within a few hours, he'd be half-asleep in a stupor on the couch in front of the picture of the Virgin Mary, five or six empty crumpled beer cans on the rickety coffee table with its plastic prosthetic leg duct-taped in place, a cigarette orange-tipped and smoking in the chunky glass ashtray. She'd be cleaning up after him, tight-lipped but unspeaking.

Ma glances over as I grab my keys off the hook. Coming home for dinner tonight?

I hope not.

It's a date?

I stick my hands in my jeans pockets and shrug, sheepish, not wanting to get into it with her. I think about how she was when Pops was here, how melancholy saturated the air, how they'd liked each other when I was small, and even joked around, but by the time he left they'd become two strangers who didn't care if the other one ever smiled again. She sets her knife down and looks intently at me, wagging her finger.

Remember, Ezekiel, to pay. Remember, girls like boys who treat them properly. Remember, don't assume anything.

I know, I know. It's not like this is my first date. What I'm thinking is, Opinions are like assholes, everyone's got 'em, but everyone knows you don't say that to your mom.

Well, she says, and pauses. It's been a few years since that girl in college, hasn't it? I never liked her, too much makeup, so much lipstick. And that smoking habit you picked up from her! You got so skinny. She was a bad, bad influence on you and you . . . wouldn't understand that. Remember how much you struggled? You dropped out of school? She clicks her tongue.

I know you never liked her, Ma. And I vape now, all right?

You know they've found out that's not good either, right? What good woman's going to want you smoking around her all the time? It's no wonder you wound up with that bad girl.

I want to say she doesn't have any business lecturing me. She and Pops can't tell me anything I don't already know from watching them, but the muscles strain around her lips and it's clear she's struggling not to say more, just hoping, wildly, I meet someone, hoping I wind up happy, not like her, alone in a cold apartment on the edge of a high desert town. At least she's chill most of the time, not stressed like she was when I was growing up, and maybe that's all either of us can expect.

I head past the dumpster to the back of the apartment building. I can feel rain coming, and I need to make sure the time machine I'm working on is fully covered by the giant black tarp. It's in a rickety shed with a chunk of roof missing. I'm jumping the gun a little, calling it a time machine. Right now, it's only a tall metal box that you can sit down in. But I managed to outfit it with a motor, some kind of technology I got downtown that the guy who sold it to me swore was a year-hopper. And a ham radio too. I can hear hams broadcast from anywhere in the desert and even listen in on conversations between astronauts on the International Space Station. A lot of cranks. Lately, people chewing on conspiracy theories about why whales have been swimming too close to the seawalls in Los Angeles, crashing into them and dying.

Late one night a few weeks ago, I heard a stargazing tour inside the park from the radio. They were talking about the gas and dust that had gathered into a nebula more than 1344 light-years away in Orion's Belt. It's a pregnant nebula, giving birth to thousands of new stars. For a moment, I wondered if I was setting my sights too low with traveling back in time with the machine. Was it possible I could travel so far into the future, none of this life would matter? A place where all those baby stars had grown up, gotten out of the nursery? But it doesn't matter, I guess, because I still haven't gotten the thing to work. Still, I cover it up. I don't want folks to mess with the keypad inside the machine—that's where you enter the year you want to go back to.

My year is back in the last century, that time when Ma and Pop and I were happy in our tiny apartment, and I felt safe, like nothing could touch us. But I've sat inside the machine with it turned on for hours, thinking hard, and it still hasn't taken me back.

In the driveway, below a raggedy hoop, a few of the Filipino kids I used to go to junior college with are playing basketball. They try to wave me over. Hey, two on two? one of them shouts.

Nah, man, I gotta see about a girl.

They start laughing and shouting. I ignore them, headed for the junky silver hatchback. I bought it used, in installments, from my weed dealer. My dealer is a strange guy, but spiritual. He never smokes with me, but he is always laughing, and I can't tell if he is laughing at me or because he is doing some cheesy laughter yoga or because he is high on edibles. I'd put in overtime at the kung fu studio, and I took another job tending bar and didn't try to meet any women. It had taken forever and a day to get this car, over a year, but once I'd fully paid it off, I thought maybe, just maybe, it would be good to date again. I went to a lady psychic with a storefront that said Life on Mars in Pioneertown. She wasn't much older than me and wore her stringy white-blonde hair gathered in a glittery purple turban with a few strings of it peeking out around her face. My dealer swore by her Tarot readings. She does 'em sober, he said. Trust. Plus, she does walk-ins, which helps when you can't keep the days entirely straight.

What I want to know, I told her, setting down my backpack and taking the mint she offered me, is whether I'm ever going to meet the one. And how will I know her?

Oh, we all want to know that, she said. Eternal questions. Let me see here. She laid down the cards and scrutinized them. They were fancy cards with gilt edges. One of them had a picture of a jester on it; he was throwing balls around in a circle and it was so realistic I could swear I saw the balls move. Another had pentacles on it. Ma would have looked at this card and said I was relying on devils and needed to cleanse my soul. My heart pounded. The psychic had been quiet for too long, picking up one card and then another, tilting her head to one side and then the other, studying them.

Is everything okay?

Yes! she said, now ecstatic, as if she were drunk on what she'd seen, and looked me straight in the eyes. She waved a card close to my face and said, The Lovers! This is a clear sign. I think you'll meet her soon. Not the ordinary way, mind you, in a grocery store or a night-school class or whatever, but on a dating app. And I'm seeing something else, too, with this other card.

She held up a faded card with three golden, winged creatures hovering around a wheel of fortune.

Which is what?

You're working on an important project, right?

Yes, I said, feeling a tug at my heart. The time machine. How did she know about the time machine? She said she was psychic, but maybe she could hear me speculating on my ham radio, the way I could hear the weird ham go on about the whales and seawalls, and once something called fog catchers.

But it's not going well, she said. You can't figure out why it's not doing what it should be doing. She squinted at a card in consternation, biting her lip, before her face relaxed and her single dimple showed again. This woman, your true love, has the information you need to complete this project. It's like how, when I moved here for the right synergy, I met my husband, a producer in Hollywood on a vacation, and after the success of his latest, he helped me open this store. When you meet this woman, the stars will align, and she'll explain how to make things work. This is the part they don't tell you. Fairy tales do happen. Life does not need to be barren.

That night I sat in my time machine and browsed the dating app the psychic had recommended, trying not to think of myself as desperate, trying not to think of what my girlfriend of five years ago would've said about people who use dating apps. Maybe what the psychic had meant was that I would find a rich person who could fund the research into my machine. No, that couldn't be it. Too easy.

I swiped right on a statuesque redhead. Valentine—it seemed like a sign that this was her name. In her profile, she wrote about loving Beat poetry, noodles for luck, and long sunset walks inside the park at Joshua Tree. Of course, everyone likes long sunset walks in the desert, and that made me pause, like did she think this detail made her seem unique? Or was she trying to seem more relatable—did she want to cast the widest possible net? Should I swim into the net? I was probably overthinking it, I told myself and typed some blather, clicked send, and pretty soon we were messaging back and forth, a volley of digital love missives. A few days later, my pulse racing, I ran by the psychic's again, and she said, yes, the stars were in the right places, and it was time to meet up.

I WAIT FOR VALENTINE in my car at a little café close to the gas station on the 62 outside the park. It was her idea to meet here. It would be more romantic if we met at one of the big piles of boulders inside the park and started our relationship scrambling through them with the sunset as our backdrop, like that represents something, getting through hardship or whatever that makes marriages stronger, but she wants to eat first. I badly need a smoke and can barely hold myself steady in the force of possibility shooting up my spine and down into my toes.

We're going to get sandwiches. Both sandwiches will involve a lot of onions and pickles, since we both are okay with breath that smells like onions or pickles—or that's what we said in the texts anyway. Honestly? I'm not wild about onion breath. It makes kissing awkward, and she's the one who brought it up, but I went along with her because she is perfect, and I need her to like me. She holds the key to making my time machine work. And if this goes well, we're going to take that trail by Barker Dam as the sun sets, and if that walk goes well, who knows, maybe she'll be my girlfriend.

But if you don't like me, just pretend you have something else going on! she'd texted.

I can't do that because you'll already know I'm lying, so I guess you're stuck with me, I texted back. Smiley face.

We flirted like this all night yesterday, until long past when I wanted to go to sleep. I feel like she really sees me, you know? She sees under the mask, and it's such a relief. When you're never seen, being seen like this just feels like the world is suddenly yours, open to your interpretations for a change. Oh, I know I haven't met her yet, but sometimes you just get a feeling, you know? We laughed at the same texts, we knew all the same references. She likes martial arts movies, and I teach kung fu. She likes to drive, and I just got a car. We both like sandwiches. We have tons in common, you know?

I'm smoking a spliff and looking out at a mural of enormous crows across the road by the pizza place when she gets off the bus. She looks just like her picture. Curves. Red hair. Cowboy hat. Tall brown boots. She's wearing dark sunglasses, and she pulls them off in this languid gesture as she saunters through the parking lot. It takes my breath away. I climb out of my car and salute her.

You Ezekiel? she asks.

Valentine?

She nods. There's awkwardness between us, a torpor that's hard to shake. Difficult to read her eyes, there's no light in them, but I don't know if she's maybe more guarded in person than by text. I did look better in my photograph, I guess. I mean, I didn't look as Tamil. I had a baseball cap on, and maybe it made my forehead look smaller, maybe it's sexier to have a smaller forehead? And you can't tell from the photograph, but probably you can in person: my nose was broken in a fight. I feel awkward and sticky, and want to run away, but she's saying, her voice a little on edge, I thought you drove?

I did, I say. I gesture at my little silver hatchback. I get nervous and tell her about choosing the car—named Abigail after my paati in India—and how I haggled to get her price down, and I had to work on the transmission even so, but now she runs so smooth, like a dream.

She's a beauty, she says in a grave voice. I want to hug her. I feel like we know each other well enough for me to do that, but I don't give in to the urge: no need to scare her. She answers the unspoken question by waving an arm gracefully at the café sign. Shall we?

Inside, I say it's on me. She doesn't answer, so I guess that's expected. You never know anymore. I went on a date a few years ago where the lady wanted to pay and seemed offended when I offered. I like how traditional Valentine is, there's something soft about her that makes me want to take her to a carnival and win her a squishy teddy bear using the impossible metal claw, and eat a chocolate sundae out of the same dish. Vanilla, if that's what she likes.

I gesture grandly at the list of sandwiches. The ponytailed guy behind the counter wears a pale tunic and looks bored; he's probably seen too many first dates to count.

I don't want to put you out, she says, pursing her red lips. Lipstick leaches into little lines near her mouth, like maybe she doesn't know entirely how to apply it, and my heart catches. Maybe it could be my job to protect her.

Oh, you're not putting me out at all, I reassure her. She starts laughing, and it's not the kindest of laughs. I suck in my breath. I'm used to people thinking I'm slow when they meet me, but I don't think this is one of those instances. Or is it? She said it so deadpan.

She orders a vegetarian sandwich with extra onions, and the man hands her the black pager as I wrack my brain trying to think if her profile said she was a vegetarian. Unable to recall, I order the same. Turkey breath while eating seems like a bad plan. My ex-girlfriend was a fruitarian, though every once in a while she gave up and ate Cheetos. It's okay to cheat sometimes, she insisted, and that made me wonder if she was talking about something bigger. She worked as a dominatrix at a club in Palm Springs, and she always looked so beautiful, but I never saw her work: she wanted to keep her lives separate. She eventually dumped me in the cruelest way, and I saw her sadistic side, that side the other men had seen and liked. When we were together, she'd loved that I wanted to look out for her, that I was protective. But by the end, she couldn't stand that I didn't think about the welfare of the chickens, like ever. I asked for another chance, but I was too slow for her, she said, and wouldn't look me in my eyes.

We sit in one of those orange plastic booths that make it seem like you're supposed to be having fun, so in a way, the mood is set right for everything to go well. Perfume wafts off her, something with flowers, but heavy on the alcohol. Her earrings are huge hoops with some kind of sparkly teardrops at the bottoms.

She glances from side to side, avoiding my eyes, like she's trying to think of something to say, and I try to think of a good story or joke, but suddenly she looks right at me and starts talking, which takes the pressure off. She's a bartender, today's her day off. She makes good tips, she says in that confident way, like the more swagger she has, the more she'll convince me. That's when I notice her nails are chipped, like she hasn't had a manicure in a while, and I can see her roots, too, under the fluorescent lights. She's a brunette under that bright bottle red. Lull in the conversation. Our sandwiches are sitting on a tray up at the counter, and I jog back up the aisle to fetch them when the pager buzzes. On the way back, I realize the jogging makes me seem weak, and I try to walk slow like maybe I don't give a fuck. She doesn't say thank you when she grabs the sandwich from me.

Have you dated a lot of people on that dating site? I ask to be polite, not because I want to know. I peel the paper off my sandwich.

Not really, she says. Her bite is dainty, and she chews slowly. I meet a lot of people, but they just aren't my type. You know?

So, who is your type? I nibble on the sandwich, trying to disguise how hungry I am.

I like men who are masculine. Men's men. Into racing cars and playing football. If there's one thing I can't stand, it's a girly man. My last boyfriend was out at the racetrack every weekend. He had a yellow Corvette.

Seriously? My voice has gone high. I ask in a lower voice, Weren't you worried he'd get hurt?

A real man can handle pain, can handle even the threat of pain. And he let me drive the car all the time.

Oh. I like football, I say softly, because I can't fake any knowledge of car racing.

What team do you root for? Her voice is neutral, but I can hear the skepticism in it, creeping in like an envelope coming unglued.

Rams, I say because it's the only team I know, but the conversation is about to run away from me, I feel it. The last time I watched football for real was about twenty years ago, when Pops still lived with us. He'd dispatch cab drivers all day, and at night he'd drink one six-pack of beer and then another, and sometimes he'd beat me around the shoulders, something about a chore I didn't do or a bad grade or whatnot, and sometimes he'd throw something across the room, but eventually, he'd collapse into snoring, his limbs splayed everywhere. I don't remember much about the games. What I remember is the sound of Pops snoring on the couch, entirely in a world of his own slumber, blue light from the TV glinting off the little gold cross around his neck. I do that sometimes now, fall asleep while watching TV and drinking beer, and I think about Pops and how narrowly I avoided his same fate. At least there are no kids watching me, nobody I take out my frustration on when life gets ridic and such. I'm alone, and it's my aloneness that makes all my decisions okay.

I teach people how to fight, which everyone should know how to do. You never know when someone might attack you, and you have to know how to defend yourself, I should know after all the times someone's beaten the shit out of me. Being able to respond to that is everything. But there was this one time in a strip mall, a group of guys jumped me, screaming slurs, kicking me in the ribs to make sure I understood how dumb and sad I was. My eye socket dislocated. A rib broken. Nose broken. It doesn't matter if you know how to fight when there are that many of them whupping your ass. Still, I like to know how to fight, for that time when it's just me and one other guy.

I take a huge bite of my sandwich, and another, scarfing down bites, washing them down with Dr Pepper.

Easy, easy, she says. She laughs, but it sounds a little judgy. We don't need to talk about football. You teach kung fu, don't you?

I nod, still chewing, my mouth full of avocado and sprouts.

So we're golden, she says. Can you teach me some moves?

Sure, I say, and relax, looking at her thin shoulders, the way the bones jut out delicately like a bird's. I smile at her, and she smiles back at me, so I guess we're good, but there's something in the way she looks just past my eyes, not into them, that makes me sad. I try to meet her gaze, but she keeps looking somewhere to the side of me. What's your favorite star? I ask, hoping this is a romantic question.

I don't know stars, she says. Are you into stars?

My favorite are the nebulas. There's one in Orion's Belt. Did you know they say that some other sentient being far off in the future might be able to see us now?

Why would they be looking at us? People are boring.

You're not, I say, trying to give her a meaningful look.

She smiles and takes another bite of huge curls of smelly red onions and lettuce, which worries me since I was hoping our first kiss would be memorable in a different sort of way, then we're silent, eating together. It's always a good sign when you feel secure enough not to talk to someone.

Ready to go to Barker Dam? she asks, standing up. She looks at herself in a makeup mirror and uses a napkin to delicately wipe mustard from the side of her mouth.

I wipe my face with a napkin, feeling a little greasy, and follow her out the door.

You're so lucky you have your own car. Her eyes light up, a little odd. This car's nothing next to a yellow Corvette. Can I test-drive it?

Sure. I hand her the keys.

We walk over to Abigail together. Sure it's okay? she asks, but she doesn't hand the keys back or anything. I think of the yellow Corvette.

Why not? You're a safe driver, aren't you?

Absolutely. She clicks the key to unlock the door and slides behind the wheel. The car smells like weed—my boys and I were hotboxing yesterday—and I hope she doesn't mind it. The backseat is cluttered with a basketball, a sheaf of papers, a couple library books, a set of compact discs so that I can learn Korean and maybe move to South Korea one day. I open the passenger door, about to get in. Can I take it out alone? she asks, blinking up at me from under long feathery lashes.

Really? Why?

Oh you know how it is, just you and the road. She smiles, and I think about how much thinking I get done when it's just me in my car—all the breakthroughs with my time machine came in those hours—and maybe she needs that. I mean, maybe I'm luckier than her that way, to have that time alone on the road while she's stuck on a dusty shuttle.

No racing, okay? I say.

She's slammed the door shut. See you in a few!

Through the open window, she looks up at me with her bright hazel eyes and grins, a flash of sweet, vulpine white teeth, and then she's easing out of the spot, and driving toward 62, steering slowly at first but then weaving past an old lady pushing a shopping cart across the road. We forgot to kiss. Hey, watch it! I call out, but she doesn't look back. She turns left at the stop sign and speeds down the highway.

I wave at her in case she's looking, I just can't see, and I lean back against another car to wait. After a few minutes, I run back into the café for a date-syrup latte. Never had one of these things, but my dealer swears by them. A line has formed, a medley of students and workers on break, all of them with heads bowed, lost in their smartphones. I check my own phone. No messages. I order two lattes, one for her, so she can see I'm a gentleman, like my mother taught me, and I wonder if my dad ever bought lattes for my mom, if he ever gave her anything but grief. Outside, clouds are rolling in, huge, white, perilously low in the sky. It's chilly, and I'm worried about seeing that sunset. I expect to see Valentine standing by my car by now, but she's nowhere to be seen.

I text Valentine. *Hey, head back now?*

No response. Maybe, driving, she hasn't noticed the text yet. I walk back to the spot where I'd parked, where another car has taken my place. I look around again more carefully to see if she's across the street or something. I can see my text message was received. The least she could do is pull over and text me back.

Rain drizzles into my latte. Light, then huge drops. I take big sips, and when the rain doesn't stop, sprint back under the overhang by the café. People are concluding their breaks, getting back into their cars. Still no text. A little clenching inside my chest. I thought we'd hit it off. Had I said something to ruin it? I review the conversation in my mind, sentence by sentence. Nothing jumps out.

I text her again. *IT'S RAINING. You heading back?*

Nothing. I look in the messages on the dating site and check my email. Nothing.

You okay? asks an older woman, hobbling by under her black umbrella.

Yeah, yeah, I'm fine.

I realize I'm drenched. And cold. Water's seeping into a hole in my sneaker, leaving my sock spongy. I'm so fucking cold. I look at the watch my ex-girlfriend had bought for me at the Dollar Store and outfitted with a gray strap. *Happy Birthday—this will help with your time management skills.* It's been an hour and a half since she left. I text again. *This isn't funny, not even a little. WHERE ARE YOU???*

There was this time, when I was pint-size, where Pops and
Ma took me to a spring carnival somewhere east of us, way out
in the desert. The glowing yellow lights of the Ferris wheel
blurred as they spun around and around in the dimming
twilight. It felt like we were at the same height as a lilac-gray
mountain in the distance. We got blue cotton candy, and they
took me up on the Ferris wheel even though it felt like my
fingers would fall off from the cold. I was afraid we'd fall, too,
but my parents looked at each other smiling, radiant, like they
liked each other over those puffy blue clouds of sugar, and it
was so weird it made me forget gravity. That moment when we
were together, under the stars, loose-limbed and spinning, was
almost entirely anomalous. As the years went by, they stopped
looking at each other at all. Time erased how they felt about
each other. Erased our experiences together like maybe they'd
never happened. Maybe it's wrong to blame time, since maybe
time isn't what erases that glowing feeling but how people
move through it, when they're looking in opposite directions.
But I've been trying to program my time machine to take me
back to that carnival, to that peace. After what the psychic
said, I'd been meaning to feel out whether Valentine had any
experience with manipulating time. So much for that. Is she
ever coming back? Maybe not.

   The strange thing is that I believed we truly liked each other.
I'm not sure whether we didn't. More importantly, I thought
Valentine liked me, after all those texts. When she smiled at me,
it seemed sincere, like the corners of her eyes got into the feeling
and everything. I don't get it. Why would you put so much effort
into meeting someone if you didn't like them?

   I think about how hard I worked for that car this last year.
Each day, I'd come home and hunker down in front of the TV
and smoke a spliff and be all right with being alone because I was

working toward something. I didn't know it then, maybe, but I was working toward that moment in the café when Valentine and I looked at each other and smiled. Now that moment is over, just like the way my parents looked at each other over my head on the Ferris wheel is over, and my stomach is churning. Why can't we make those moments last? I picture her on a boulder at Barker Dam, the sky turning fiery as she climbs. The sound of coyotes. The intense glow behind the Joshua trees—as if the future is calling from light-years away.

KEEPING SCORE

THE COUPLE INSTALLED THE APP on their phones on a Friday night over Guinness and nachos, and later, when the dust had settled, they'd wonder at their blissful, affectionate carelessness—why hadn't they known? John microwaved shreds of sharp cheddar cheese in a Pyrex dish, while Anjalena sat cross-legged on the couch, watched the crimson icon as it slowly appeared on the cell phone screen. A small square morphing from black to color, a sun rising. The app had received press, high-end press at that, but it was only ninety-nine cents, and there was no subscription fee.

Even so, Anjalena was impatient. Younger than John by a couple of years, she'd grown up with computers and nearly everything else at her feet, even though her childhood had been darkened by her father's erratic fits of rage and her mother's cool absences. This installation is taking forever, she groaned. She touched the icon again, as if her touch would make it download faster. She knew it was futile, and yet there was something satisfying about the extra touch, the delicate press of a fingertip, just as there was pleasure, the electric jolt of dopamine, in repeatedly pushing the button for a green light when the red light at an intersection seemed to be taking too long. She touched the icon again. Her nails needed a fill, and she wondered if John, so preoccupied by his own appearance, had noticed or cared.

Touching the screen over and over won't make it download any faster. Maybe plug the phones in? John suggested as he poured melted cheese over the tortilla chips. He stood at the breakfast bar in his clean white undershirt beneath a fluorescent light that rendered all his features harsh and his dark hair a little wispy over his gleaming scalp. She was receiving a glimpse, though she didn't know it, of what he'd look like years hence, after sliding noiselessly into the night of old age.

I mean, it might just be a defective app, she said.

Would all your friends be installing it if it were defective? he asked reasonably.

A headboard upstairs began thudding gently against the drywall, their neighbors having sex. She plugged the cell phones into an electrical outlet and turned on a jazz record. Pharoah Sanders's sheets of sound drowned out the persistent beat of the headboard.

He carried the nachos out of the kitchen on a platter. The tortilla chips, stuck up at all angles like sails, were piled with roasted red peppers, jalapeños, fresh cilantro, leftover roast chicken. He set them on the crate they used as their coffee table.

He smiled, gesturing at the phones. How ridiculous are we?

Sooooo absurd. She thought quickly, not wanting him to change his mind about installing the app. But, you know, I read this article where the couples they interviewed said it made their relationships better. They said it allowed them to see themselves more clearly, and with an objective record of their behavior, they treated each other better. It was better than couples counseling, even, someone said. Cheaper too. Anyway, what could it hurt? She grabbed a chip and loaded it with chicken.

There are so many sponsored posts in magazines these days, though, so who knows?

Gah! I know right? And no doubt this was made by awful tech bros. Maybe we're stupid for downloading their app and giving them more money. She picked up her phone from the frayed arm of the couch and glanced at its face. Anyway, it's ready.

They touched the screens in time with each other, a toast.

The app was modestly designed. A brown crinkly paper background with dark red

Courier font. *Keeping Score* the splash screen announced. Personable, pleasant, nonthreatening. On the next page of the app, there was a notebook interface into which you could type everything you'd done for your partner, for the relationship. The algorithm would take your entry, cogitate, and spit out a number value.

You did the night's dishes [+1]. You cleaned a sink overflowing with the last week of dishes [+3]. You did the laundry [+2]. You brought fresh lilacs home every day for the two weeks they bloomed [+3]. You worked overtime so that there would be money for an anniversary dinner [+10]. You cleaned the litterbox [+2]. You fed the cats [+1]. You paid for the guy to come out and fix the clogged toilet [+1]. You swallowed your pride [+2]. You went along to a dinner with your significant other's ex, during which it was clear the ex still carried a torch for your significant other [+10]. You baked a cake [+5] and frosted it in buttercream [+10]. You roasted a chicken [+3]. You ate your minor, but noteworthy, criticism in order to protect your partner's ego [+7]. You attended the most boring company party on earth and smiled throughout as if you were having big fun [+5].

The app didn't limit itself to quantifying love. There was also a button that took you to another page on which you could record anything your partner did that pushed you over the edge. The algorithm would process a partner's complaint and subtract from the existing record of love. You lost varying numbers of points for every relationship failure: Your partner forgot to put the toilet seat down [-1]. Your partner forgot to pick up paper towels [-1]. Your partner allowed his OCD to overwhelm him so that he reorganized the shelves until you couldn't find anything and had to buy the lost items again. [-5]. Your partner refused to watch that arthouse film with you [-2]. Your partner hung up without saying I love you [-3]. Your partner threw out a sentimental memento because it was taking up too much room on the mantelpiece [-3]. Your partner threw out mail in a big batch and missed your partner's paycheck buried within it [-5]. Your partner failed to do the dishes [-1]. Your partner failed to write a love note and pack it with the sandwich and chips in the brown paper bag lunch [-1]. Your partner cheated on you with a stranger [-50]. Your partner cheated on you with your best friend and his wife [-100].

You know I'm going to win this. Spoken with the brash overconfidence of a former jock not fully cognizant that the glory years were behind him. He kept scrolling.

Oh please. She grabbed a cheese-covered chip and threw it at him. He laughed. She pulled a face. You're so dead.

He plucked the chip from his shirt and ate it. Well, here goes nothing then. If you're sure you can take the loss. He sipped his beer reflectively.

Keep dreaming. Remember how cocky you were about board games when we first started dating? You'd never played with anyone smart before. I wiped the floor with you.

AND SO IT BEGAN. That night, John absentmindedly left a few nachos on the china platter in the sink instead of rinsing it, which made it more difficult to wash off the hardened cheese drizzles the next morning. Negative points. But after they watched the movie she'd wanted to watch, she wouldn't go down on him, even though she'd promised to do so last time, and he sensed she was exacting a punishment for the hardened cheese drizzles, and so she lost three points, putting her at negative three.

However, the following morning, both woke eager to love each other to death. There was a beautiful love note in calligraphy in his brown paper bag, and his favorite turkey on rye with Havarti cheese and sprouts. He sexted Anjalena during her lunch hour, trying to think about what turned her on, instead of saying what he wanted to say, and she orgasmed three times. He left the middle school where he taught gym and coached five minutes early so he could meet her at her office and grab a drink before riding the metro home together. At dinner, he turned on a Thelonious record: he couldn't stand dissonant jazz, but she loved it. He rubbed her shoulders with medium pressure, digging in at her blades, like he was trying to excavate something she'd buried. When she reminded him about the massage therapy classes they had been planning to take together, he didn't grumble that she was taking a random joke he'd made over dinner and turning his playful determination to please her with the promise of massages into a chore— what she wound up doing with all of his suggestions.

She took out the guitar and serenaded him. Her singing voice was ethereal, quavering like smoke. It brought tears to his eyes, as it had the night they'd met over green tea matcha at an open mic in the neighborhood coffee shop. It was the whole reason he'd asked her out: the aphrodisiac of song, the way she'd teetered at the edge of the stool, leaning a little

too far forward on that tall stool, as if she were willing to risk
falling just to pluck those ukulele strings. His memory of her
fragility that night had bolstered him through her early rejections of his overtures. Maybe even made those rejections
somehow more meaningful. She just didn't know *yet* that they
were meant to be, but of course, she would. He'd fallen in love
with the certitude of planets, the infinite beauty of whales, a
jackhammer to the gut.

She rubbed his bare feet with peppermint lotion while he
read Bolaño out loud. He was good at doing voices and they
lost track of time. After midnight, she went to wash her hands
and light scented candles. I've been thinking about fucking
you since lunchtime, she said, and she meant it.

For a tumultuous, excited week, they entered their griev-
ances and bright spots with the diligence they usually reserved
for career advancement. Almost every action could be described
as help or hindrance. And the app provided choices. You could
calculate your scores as they were entered, a running tally, or
you could wait for a week or choose some other interval to have
the app do the math automatically, or you could manually press
a flame-colored button to tally the score at a time you and your
partner found mutually convenient. Anjalena pointed out a tiny
crimson warning at the bottom of the page that said a running
tally could get in the way of the relationship, and she insisted
that they not keep one.

I want us to just behave normally, she said. Just act normal,
so we can receive a true score, not some false score we've managed to engineer because we have a blow-by-blow we adjust to
accordingly.

Just to play devil's advocate, he said, even though he knew
she despised the phrase, it might be better for our relationship
because then we can choose to improve as we go along.

It would be annoying to have the score in my face all the time, she said. Any intelligent person would find it annoying. She spoke with a determined tone, her jaw jutting forward. He knew better than to disagree.

In spite of agreeing to tally only once a week, they privately kept track of their points and found themselves competing every day to see who could score more. Their gestures grew ever grander. The failures kept to a minimum, only the odd oversight. The weeks passed in a flurry of competitive love.

ONE SATURDAY MORNING, AFTER she'd returned from picking up everything bagels, they sat cross-legged on the love seat they'd gotten at an estate sale up the coast and recorded what they'd done for each other the night before. They clicked the flame-colored button to tally the points at the same time, and sucked in their breaths, watching the clock symbol in the corner of the screen while the algorithm processed the week's entries.

Their phones chimed at the same time. A score returned: 25:15. What is this shit? Anjalena said. How are you this far ahead of me?

He smirked. Well, you know. I do a lot.

You don't do more than me.

He started to laugh, but seeing she was coldly serious, frowned and announced firmly, I do a lot.

She left the room, slamming the door, and he felt the familiar lurch. Slamming doors made him think of his childhood, his parents' heated quarrels, of how his heart had ached all through his childhood at the anger of that slamming, wood on wood, basketball the only escape. She knew he felt that way, why didn't she stop with that shit? She only did it out of spite.

He typed it out: *slammed the door*. Only [-1], but entering the wrong soothed him. Circumspect, he took out his laptop and began working. He heard her slam the front door as she left the apartment. He exhaled forcefully, trying to let out the stress. Another [-1].

An hour later, Anjalena returned and began puttering around the kitchen: the sounds of a knife against the cutting board, a steady sizzling sound. The smoke detector gave a single, plaintive little beep. A few minutes later, she came into the bedroom with oysters fried in tamarind sauce; she'd probably gotten fresh ones from the seafood market on her walk. Her dinner parties featuring South Indian dishes with which she'd grown up were legendary among their friends. She'd adorned the plate with a garnish of fresh parsley also from the farmers market presumably.

I'm sorry. I shouldn't have slammed the door. Her shoulders slumped and her expression was contrite.

He took the plate without a word but wracked with guilt. It was too late to delete his complaints from the app. The complaints were lodged for eternity, or until the phone went through electronic recycling. She threw him a tiny conciliatory smile. I'm going to the library, she said.

After she left the apartment again, he entered the tamarind oysters into the app, holding his breath and hoping the points she'd receive would put the score back the way it was, obscuring the earlier complaints, so she wouldn't notice. She had a quicksilver temper. She'd be distraught if she registered how quickly he'd entered her door slamming. The complaints alone would surely lead to her enacting some other behavior he found stressful and she found expressive, like the screaming of obscenities. But shit, what if going to the market for fresh oysters put her ahead of him? He felt a little frantic assessing the litany of wrongs they'd listed over the past week, his breath catching at the sight, the weighty list confronting him. After a few minutes of review—he'd circumvent the algorithm in secret, if necessary—he found his score was likely still higher than hers and his body softened, his limbs loosened.

ANJALENA STROLLED PAST THE fire station to the library. She studied the last two days on the app. So he'd entered the tamarind oysters, and she'd gotten three points for it. But scrolling up, she noticed he'd entered her slamming the door. Twice. Slamming the door! Big deal. It was a tiny thing, and the algorithm recognized that: [-1]. But it was the way he'd phrased the complaint that irked her. *She slammed the door, and she knows I hate that because of my childhood trauma.* Trauma! As if a divorce were a trauma. She thought of her own father's rages—every single day of her childhood had felt apocalyptic because she hadn't known whether he would be upset that she'd left her backpack on the table instead of taking it to her room or had committed some other minor act of forgetfulness. John's parents were solid and a little steely in their cashmere and pearls and wool and pinstripe ties, but not in any way frightening.

At the library, she returned the book she'd borrowed and wandered the stacks aimlessly, not wanting to return home. She looked at the phone again and noticed he'd added several more items: she'd made the beds, she'd given him another foot massage. The complaints about slamming the doors had disappeared up the list. He was trying to game the system and hoping she wouldn't notice. She typed a quick entry. Without checking out any books, she headed back to the apartment.

AN HOUR LATER, JOHN heard the front door open. He shouted, Hey, should we have an early supper? No answer. Intentional? He shouted again. Silence. Irritated now, he typed the silent treatment into his phone—he was going to win. She'd made an entry while at the library: he sulked when *I* handed him the tamarind oysters and didn't say thank you.

He turned to his work on his laptop again. The afternoon light faded, and he switched on a lamp. Had she made dinner without him? He went out to the living room. It smelled like marinara. Garlic. The air conditioning was on, and he walked over and switched it off. He made a mental note to enter that: she knew he didn't want an outrageous bill. At first, he didn't see her there in the dark, but as his eyes adjusted, he realized she was huddled on the couch eating over her bowl of pasta.

Hey, any left for me?

You gonna say thank you this time? Her voice was sarcastic and mean. He leaned closer and realized from the smell of her breath she was drinking. In the dim light, he made out a balloon glass full of gin on the crate.

I'm sorry, he said lightly. I didn't know it would piss you off that much.

You knew. You always do this phony innocent shit. She picked up the balloon glass and took a sip.

He flicked on the light, and she blinked and rubbed her eyes. He shrugged. I honestly didn't think about it. Thank you?

You never think. She scowled and blinked furiously, her eyes tearing.

He sighed loudly and went to the pantry. There was a can of tomato soup. He took the lid off and poured the runny orange-red into the saucepan. He turned up the flame and waited for it to boil.

And remember to do the dishes, she snapped, before disappearing into the shadowy bedroom.

LACERATING SILENCE MARKED the following week. They recorded failures to wash dishes or to fold laundry, but they barely spoke. Each cursed the other, below their breath. Each typed blame into the app. It spit out numbers. Back and forth, they seesawed.

Should we tally on Friday night this week? she asked in a monotone, not expecting much. She'd tamped down on her emotions, careful of how he interpreted their tenor and volume. He was equally flat when he responded yes.

The end of the week came and with it, the inevitable slowing. The chance to face all the anxiety and disappointment that had blurred over accumulated minutes. Laundry had piled up around the apartment. Shirts and boxer shorts and dresses in piles, exuding the stench of inattention. They'd both imagined the score-keeping app would make life easier—easier, anyway, to navigate their relationship—but a strangling rhythm of cranky accusations had overwhelmed them both.

Well, did you log it correctly? There's no way I'm higher than you on failure to wash dishes.

Excuse me? You never do the dishes! Do you think some magic fairy comes out of the woodwork to do these dishes you can't even be bothered to rinse? It's me, I'm the fucking dish-washing fairy.

RECORDING COMPLAINTS HAD BECOME a kind of addiction, a way to release energy that had previously been spent in breath: talking and making up and talking and making up. By the month's end, both had fallen into negative terrain on the app, but this time John had fallen farther than Anjalena. For the third or fourth time, while they ate dinner, she jumped the gun and tallied the score herself as if she had a better understanding of what the app had calculated than he did. You're losing—you know that, right? she announced, for the third or fourth time, as they sat on the couch watching a TV show he liked. Her voice was cold, mildly sneering. She knew a perverse pleasure in using this tone. In her gut, she suspected it was the one she'd use after they'd been married too long.

Look, doesn't that mean we're both losing? he tried.

You could interpret it that way, I guess. Or maybe you could refrain from dragging me to

your level. Another bitter laugh. She picked up a heap of his dirty clothes that was so tall it hid her face, and with an exaggerated show of exertion, heaved it into the plastic basket.

Why don't we tally? Get the exact numbers? We're just guessing right now. He grabbed her sweater from the back of the couch and pointedly dropped it in the basket. He stalked over to the record player and turned off Thelonious.

She sighed. Fine. They walked toward each other in the living room, each clicking the tally button. They stared into each other's eyes, hers brown and long-lashed and round, his gray, deep-set, and narrow, each willing the other to look away.

The phones dinged. The app was finished calculating. They looked down at their phones at the same time.

I was right, she said.

Okay, fine, but wouldn't you rather be loved than right? He shut off the phone sharply.

That's your problem, don't you see? You make no effort. You assume someone will love you just the way you are. She went into the kitchen and began looking in the cabinets as if certain she'd find something new there.

Not *somebody*. You! I mean, I thought you did love me. Otherwise, what are we even doing? He followed her, stood by the stove. From the upstairs apartment, they heard the slow and steady thumps of the headboard banging.

She swung around with a cry. I can't be the one doing all the work all the time. You think because you grew up with women fawning all over you for no reason that you don't need to try.

No reason? No reason? I'm a good boyfriend. I've never had a girlfriend who was lazier in a relationship than you.

Lazy? You're one to talk. There's more to life than being a college basketball star, and if you'd ever held down a real job, you'd know that. Sorry if I have more important things to do than make you feel—

A real job? So you're successful in capitalism, how does that make your job more important than mine?

Spoken like a loser. Anjalena's face crumpled as she said it, defeated by her own worst instincts. Tears streamed down her face. Minutes ticked by, with the shouts of exuberant sex from upstairs. It would have made them laugh, ordinarily.

I don't want to fight. John touched her arm. Want to catch a movie this weekend?

He'd meant it to sound like a pickup line, as if they were back in the early throes, her nearly falling off the stool as she took the green tea matcha. As the words left his mouth, he realized the tone was off. Whining, weak, already deflated, already painfully aware that however close they stood in the cramped kitchen, his heart had drifted away like a planet away from the sun, its gravitational pull diminishing more with each passing minute.

She sighed heavily and wiped her eyes. He resisted the urge to wipe her tear-streaked face. Her voice nearly broke as she asked, Should we make dinner?

Sure. Salad?

She rolled her eyes. Salad again?

He took out the lettuce and began chopping, quickly, chef strokes from back when he'd worked in the kitchen of the French restaurant down the street. He hoped she'd notice how he'd tried to ease the mood, how he'd ignored her eye roll, how he'd forgotten already the contempt that animated her every withering glance.

She took out tomatoes, red peppers, a Vidalia onion, pepperoncini. Glossy, unblemished vegetables. Croutons. Their upstairs neighbors were quiet now. The sound of the knife against the cutting board and the rustle of plastic and paper were punctuated by the occasional footstep.

You want to put the garlic bread in the oven? he asked.

Wordlessly, she took the leftover loaf from the refrigerator and set it on a baking tray.

You might preheat the oven first, he said. He'd meant to be helpful, but she frowned.

He finished chopping the vegetables and threw them together in a salad bowl.

She turned on the TV, but as they sat together at the small round table, staring at

their phones quietly, desperately, neither paid the slightest attention to the show. A red rose wilted in a bud vase in the center of the table, the single point he'd scored that week.

Are you going to record the salad I made?

You going to record the garlic bread?

Jesus. All the garlic bread involved was throwing it in the oven, he said helplessly.

What do you mean? It was from scratch, butter and freshly chopped garlic and the rest of that parsley. Let's just see what the app says, since, after all, you trust it more than you trust me.

Why are you taking that tone with me?

What tone?

I went along with you by installing that stupid app in the first place, didn't I? I didn't have any interest in keeping score, or changing our relationship, but of course, you always have to do what your friends are doing. God forbid we ignore the noise and do our own thing.

Everything this app tallies, I've asked you to fix before. I wanted you to install the app so that you would try. You don't try! Despair entered her voice. You don't try as hard as I do, and you don't even care.

All I fucking do is try these days, but you're impossible. You do know that, don't you? Who do you think is going to love you with your standards? His heart sank, not entirely sure he meant the words but wanting her defeat.

You perform for show, that's not the same as really trying. Her face stayed smooth.

Rage came over John, hot, blinding, sweet, red. He hurled his phone across the room with all his might. It shattered against the metal bookshelf, glass and plastic and copper and silver flying. The pieces fell into a sparkling, jagged mosaic on the hardwood floor. He scooted his salvaged wingback chair back a little, evidently startled.

Anjalena smiled, not missing a beat, and picked up her cell phone. She typed deliberately with her index finger, every touch of the screen a jolt of pleasure.

Oh my god, really? Put that phone down, he shouted. Put it the fuck down! Fuck! Fuck!

She continued to type.

I'll do a final tally and then we'll see. She pressed the flame-colored button with a resolute air of smugness. Moments later, the cheerful sound rang out from her phone. See? I was right.

He grabbed the phone from her, seized with a fury neither had known he possessed. She paused and then began laughing helplessly, jaggedly, as if she didn't know what else to do, but instead of joining her, as he might have in days of yore, this only enraged him more. He threw the phone from the window into the canyon, the app dinging sweetly again and again in a relentless victory.

A MINOR DISTURBANCE

JEISY HADN'T MET THE LODGER. She'd never placed an advertisement in the newspaper, nor arranged for his arrival, but there was a spacious, furnished spare room with a large window that faced west, and he settled in without much fuss, a mere shadow whose presence changed the house's energy only minutely. Perhaps if he'd come with more fanfare, Jeisy would have been disturbed and promptly kicked him out. But he arrived over the weekend, or at least that's when they first heard the sound of his luggage lightly bumping and rolling behind his thudding footsteps. From the dining table, they heard the creak of the door and looked at each other, puzzled, uncertain about what to do.

Should we say hello? Jeisy's oldest daughter, Antolina, asked as she stirred her rice and vegetables.

Jeisy frowned, her eyebrows drawing together. She crossed her arms, unsure. I suppose we should. Or maybe we should wait until your father comes home. He probably arranged it before the expedition and forgot to tell me.

After doing the dishes, the four of them tiptoed down the long dark hall. The house made a huge cracking sound, and then settled on its foundation with a near sigh. Jeisy held the toddler by the hand, noticing how sweaty with dread he was. At the end, a thin line of faint light shone under the door of the spare room, but when Antolina knocked, nobody answered. She knocked again, rapping three times. Jeisy shrugged at her.

They assumed they would see the lodger the next day at breakfast or dinner. Later in the week, they looked around the kitchen, curious about what he ate, as if food might serve as a clue about who he was, but he hadn't brought any food. Nevertheless, there were traces of him. He'd rearranged the cereal boxes. He'd left out a clean dish as if he'd planned to eat, but changed his mind and forgot to put it back in its cabinet above the counter.

While Jeisy took her youngest to a preschool music class, and Antolina and Noel went to a friend's house to hang out and do god knows what, he must have come out. When the family approached the front door upon their return, they heard the TV running. They expected to find him sprawled out in the living room, but he was nowhere to be seen. As far they could tell, he'd been watching some terrible afternoon talk show while eating chips. Tiny potato-colored crumbs flecked the black leather couch like dandruff.

In the evenings, hoping to catch a glimpse of the lodger, the girls hovered by his door, sniffing. The scents shifted slightly. Shoe polish, leather, yeast, lilacs, rain. It wasn't a perfectly masculine odor, not like the way Noel's room gave off a teenage smell, but something more muddled. Perhaps the lodger wasn't even a man, despite the heavy footfalls on the first night. Sometimes they heard him pace around the room, but it was mostly silent, like he knew they were listening.

He showered in the bathroom across from his room when they weren't home. They hadn't used the bathroom in years, but once when Antolina listened at his door, she noticed water droplets leading from the bathroom door to his door. Jeisy had gone down to investigate the bathroom. Sure enough, the air was humid, forgotten, and opaque, and sudsy water pooled at the bottom of the tub. Several damp guest towels were strewn over the tile floor.

Does he expect us to do his laundry? she grumbled loudly as she picked up the towels, half hoping he would hear her. She opened the medicine cabinet, but there was nothing inside other than what a long-ago lodger—who'd vacated the room when Antolina was still a baby—had left behind.

NEARLY A WEEK ROLLED by with no sign of the lodger beyond the traces he left behind, Jeisy grew uneasy. She was alone in a house in the mountains with three children. He could be anybody. He could be someone off the street. Somehow, in the mystery that surrounded him, he'd acquired an odd power over her, over the house. She resolved to ask her husband to whom he'd rented the room during their upcoming weekly call.

She avoided thinking about the inevitable confrontation with her husband; he should have told her he'd rented out the room before he'd left on the expedition. But she began worrying that he had told her, and she was the one who hadn't been paying attention. She didn't want to confront him; she had to confront him. Worry welled up inside her, hot and perplexing until the moment she heard her husband's voice on the landline. It sounded scratchy and far away. She thought of him cold and shivering among the polar ice caps. Snow surrounding him, snow on this line. He was in such an expansive and empty place that their confusion would seem minor in comparison. She'd told him to find someone to move in, hadn't she? She should be more generous about his forgetfulness.

So who is this person you rented the room to?

What? I'm sorry about that. I never did find a lodger.

He was playing a prank on her. He'd done that a lot early in their marriage. He'd pretend to fall off a boulder when he was simply jumping to a lower flat rock. He'd had a cactus delivered in place of a Christmas tree one year. Now when he was away and they were apart, they were sometimes more like they'd been in those times. Stop joking, she said. Did you check his references?

Seriously, I couldn't find anyone. We'll need to post another ad when I get back.

Then, who is that person living in the room down the hall?

Are you turning the tables on me? That isn't funny. I'm nearly nine thousand miles away.

Atoms of electric dread shifted inside Jeisy's body. I'm dead serious. He's down the hall now, but I've never met him.

How did he get into the house?

It seemed like something she should know. I'm not sure, but he seems harmless? The most he does is rearrange the furniture.

Well, ask for rent, at least. We're not running a charity.

Asking the lodger to pay rent was a reasonable request. The safest way was to go down the hall one afternoon while the children were at school. The next day, though it was overcast outside and the house dark, there was no light under the door, but she could hear shuffling inside the room. She knocked. Knocked again. Are you there? We never arranged the rent.

More shuffling sounds. And then a creak, as if someone had sat down on the chair in front of the window. She tried the door handle. It was locked. Her frustration came to the surface.

I need to talk to you!

Another creak.

You can't just live here rent-free, you know. My husband will be home, and he'll wonder why you've stayed.

The following week, two days before Jeisy's husband was supposed to return from the expedition, he called and said he'd need to take an extra week away. Her heart sank. You'll be back when? Next Friday?

I'm sorry. How are you doing there? Do you and the kids need me home?

No, I know, if they're asking you to do it . . . Jeisy glanced around the room, her ear cocked, as it always was now, to hear whether the lodger had left his room.

I'll be back soon, he said.

Perhaps the lodger had been somewhere down the hall listening to her side of the conversation, because as the days passed, he grew bolder. Unseen, he alphabetized the bookshelves in the living room. He moved the radio on the coffee table out of reach to a higher shelf. He replaced pictures: the sedate painting of bay stallions on the dining room wall was exchanged for a surreal collage featuring a narwhal. The silk roses on the dining table were replaced with velvet pansies. One day while Jeisy was picking the children up from school, the huge wooden cross with golden tips was carried away from the foyer. She stared at the discolored wall where the cross had been, its image branded upon the wood. When the children scattered to their respective rooms to do their homework, she paused at the entryway of the living room. It hardly seemed her own living room.

Bit by bit, Jeisy's life, so orderly, so scheduled, so meticulously planned, was turned over. On a daily basis, she thought of confronting the lodger, but weeks passed, and she couldn't figure out how to confront him properly. Her husband's job had extended his stay—they'd discovered ancient hills and rivers strangely well-preserved beneath an ice sheet—and during each weekly call, he asked if she'd managed to kick the lodger out yet.

I'm waiting for you to come home. You can do it.

I don't like to think of you alone in that house with a stranger, her husband said.

Well then, come home, she said.

The children were used to their father's long absences, and the house ticked on with its familiar clockwork. Yet, the lodger's unseen presence seemed to change the very air that they breathed inside their own house. It was not their own anymore: all the molecules were rearranged. Sometimes when they returned home after being away for a few hours, the house no longer smelled like their own familiar spices, but like something colder, more piquant.

Her children never asked any questions, but Jeisy felt they must notice the strangeness, that their house was transforming before them. She went down the hall, the light under the door visible, and knocked. Silence, as she'd expected—dreaded. She turned on the hallway light: two of the three incandescent bulbs were blown out, and the hall remained dim, a permanent twilight. Shuffling and rustling sounds arose from inside the room. She couldn't help her tone, pugilistic, forbidding. You there?

The doorknob was cold to the touch. Slowly she turned it, willing it to be locked so that she wouldn't see anything she didn't want to see. The door was locked.

An irrational panic gripped her. She tried to turn the knob again, as if she'd get a different result. Her heart sunk with the enormity of what was happening. He couldn't just live in the house uncommunicative, without paying rent, without respecting the furnishings and the pictures. Propelled by pure icy anger, she turned the doorknob again and again, senselessly.

Open the door! she shouted, her breath ragged. Open the damn door! It's our door, not yours. Tears of frustration formed in her eyes.

Mommy, are you okay? Aaron was standing in his yellow pajamas with owl feet in the dim hallway, blinking, his nubby baby blanket he'd dragged with him strewn on the floor behind.

She sucked in her breath and wiped her eyes. I'm sorry. I'm okay, kutty. Let's go back to your room.

He clutched her clammy hand with his tiny, hot, sweaty fingers. They traveled the long narrow hallway to the other end of the house, and she sent him to the bathroom to pee again while she turned down the covers on his bed. When he returned and crawled into his bed, she sat at the edge, and held his hand, keeping an ear cocked for sounds elsewhere in the house. I'm scared, can you sleep with me? Aaron asked.

Just for a few minutes, she whispered. She was still listening for sounds, wondering if the lodger would come charging through the shadows in the hall. She could hear the quiet sounds of her other children in their rooms nearby: Antolina on the phone, Noel playing video games. She flung an arm around Aaron and as she held him close, his breathing changed, quickened, the feel of him breathing as if they were the same person, until she strained to hear her other children beyond the immediate sounds of his shallow breaths.

SHE WOKE THE NEXT morning before anyone was up and un-wrapped herself from Aaron, quietly padding down the hall and past the sliding glass doors of the living room, glimpsing a dreamy pink light percolating through the yuzu tree, and feeling uncertain about whether she was ready to shake things up with the lodger and spoil the peace of those early hours. She moved across the room to the hall and then stood for a moment at the lodger's door and tried not to let herself breathe as quickly as she and Aaron had the night before. Damp air was drifting out of the bathroom across from his door. She pushed the bathroom door open gently and felt the warm droplets of water on the air. So he'd had a shower. She returned to stand by his door again. I know you're in there, she announced loudly, with more confidence than she felt. You can't stay in there forever and eventually you'll have to come out.

LATER THAT DAY, AFTER she'd made breakfast for the older children and sent them to a friend's house to play, she received a call from her husband's phone unexpectedly. A fizz of anxiety arose in her, and when she heard the voice on the other end, a baritone she'd heard many times at her husband's office parties, she knew immediately the news would be upsetting. She muted the TV and perched on the edge of the couch. She willed the news to be somehow okay.

I'm so sorry, Jeisy, ma'am. Your husband has disappeared.

When? Her grip tightened on her phone.

A week ago, he went out with a few others across the sea ice to Petermann Island. It was supposed to be a one-day trip to collect samples to compare to the ones from the eastern ice sheet, but a storm blew in and disrupted the ice, and they weren't able to return. He paused, as if to let this much of the news sink in.

When the ice was in place, we went out there, he said. Yesterday and again today. We searched but couldn't find them.

You'll go out again, won't you?

We will go out one more time, he said carefully. But we've made a thorough sweep.

Jeisy hung up with a deep shudder. She thought of her husband buried in the snow. Was the last conversation they'd had about the lodger? She wished she could go back and have the conversation again and talk about the children, reminisce about the day they'd met, the day they'd married. Why did their last conversation have to center that fucking lodger?

There had always been risks to his work. They'd always known, but somehow the possibility of stones, the possibility of a crevasse, had never felt real. He'd never had a colleague die. Now he was the colleague who died. Her whole body felt icy, as if she were alone in a snowstorm, naked, unguarded. She couldn't stop shivering.

She went through the motions of making dinner and talking to the children about what they'd done at school. None of them suspected anything was amiss. When she tucked Aaron in, he flopped over without asking her to stay as he had the night before. His cheeks had less baby fat. It felt like her heart was vibrating, like maybe her body could sense, even from all this distance, her husband's body, lost somewhere on the ice floes, his spirit abandoning his body; one day, he would be like those rivers and hills, preserved under the ice, and she, too, would go, disappearing under her ceaseless anxiety, the long, steady bleed of it for the rest of her life. In the living room, the TV played on while she thought only of him, before she got to her feet, shut it off, and—all of it out of habit—retired to her room.

THE FOLLOWING MORNING, WHEN Jeisy returned to the house after dropping the kids off at school, she opened the front door and saw that the house had been put asunder. The couch was overturned, cushions yanked out. The chairs stood on end like animals on their backs. Pictures had been torn from the walls, leaving patches where they'd hung. Silk flowers were shredded and strewn on the living room carpet and at the edge of the adjacent dining room, with the white breakfast bowls still sitting on the table from when the children had eaten pancakes there. The dahlias she bought every week at the market cascaded across the soaked tablecloth and spilled onto the floor in pink ecstasy. She didn't even bother to close the front door but raced into the dining room with a cry. Like a madwoman, she ran among the capsized furniture and pictures and flowers, kicking and flailing with so much abandon anyone might have thought she was dancing. Her head was empty but for the revenge. She wanted revenge for the house, for the way in which this lodger had taken it over as if it were his own.

Jeisy charged down the hall and pounded on the door until her fists were sore. Let me in, let me in! You can't ruin our home like this!

She crumpled to the floor and stared at the door for hours, willing it to open. She could hear the faintest rustling. The lodger did not take her seriously.

Jeisy thought about her husband, about how they'd chosen this house together just before Antolina was born. They were scheduled to have a call at the end of the week, after he'd finished collecting samples out on the ice. She took out her cell phone and scrolled through her contacts. She thought about fetching a neighbor. But the thought of revealing that she'd simply allowed this lodger to take over the house? She didn't know how she would explain the weeks that had passed.

She considered calling the police, but ever since a run-in with two diligent rent-a-cops in her teenage years, she'd feared and mistrusted them. It seemed so violent to involve the police, like she was spoiling for a fight. It would escalate matters, take the quarrel with the lodger into unknown territory. And the police might blame her too. What would she say about how the lodger had gotten into the house? Perhaps they would think she'd invited the lodger, or else why would he show up, so brazen. She rose and went back to the living room, unsure of where to start cleaning up.

After hours confronted with such disorder, she swallowed her pride and called the police. The woman who took her information sounded like she'd just been woken up. Her questions stretched out, seemingly interminable. Jeisy clutched the phone to her ear as she answered them.

The dispatcher sent an officer who arrived twenty minutes later. He looked soft from suburban life, his gut hanging comfortably over his pants. He walked in and looked around. She'd managed to clean up the dahlias and mop up the spilled water. She'd picked up the silk petals, and she handed them to him. This is what he did! The room was still visibly disturbed.

Your lodger did all this? the officer asked. His eyebrows were raised in skepticism. Did you see him doing it?

Well, no. I mean I came home, and it was like this.

I can't assume it was him. Are there any signs of forced entry?

No, I don't think so. She shrugged helplessly.

He went from door to door and checked the windows. Look, he said, your sliding glass door is unlatched.

One of the children probably just forgot to close it, Jeisy said.

He took out some equipment and began patting at the sides of the door. Dusting for fingerprints, he explained.

Don't you want to check down the hall? That's where he is.

Just a minute. He put something into a baggie.

I'm sure nobody broke in, Officer.

You never can be too careful. If I were you, I'd check all the entrances to the house were locked before going out.

She led him down the hall to the lodger's room. He knocked. It's the police, sir.

You see? He won't let you in. He's unreasonable.

The officer turned the doorknob and tried to push the door open. If he doesn't want to be disturbed, that's that, he said.

You can't be serious. There's nothing you can do?

The officer shrugged. You could evict him, I guess. Anyway, you catch him messing things around again, you give us a call.

When the officer left, there were still a few hours before she would need to pick up the kids from school. She searched for a lawyer using her phone and called a solo practitioner who specialized in landlord-tenant issues. His secretary patched her through to the lawyer. He sounded like an elegant gentleman; in his voice she heard tobacco and Scotch and a whisper of silk. She explained about the lodger, how he'd appeared one day and gradually changed the entire house, and now she needed to get rid of him as quickly as possible.

You never signed a rental agreement? That does put you in a bind, the lawyer said. Now there was judgment in his voice, as if she'd done something wrong in not meeting the lodger.

I never met him. He just showed up and took over that room without a word. He never comes out, except when we're gone. He ruined the living room. The police thought I might evict him.

But you haven't seen him? Do you know if he ever comes out of that bedroom?

He must. He takes showers in a bathroom across the hall.

I can draw up the paperwork, but you'd need to serve him.

After they hung up, Jeisy felt a weight had been lifted from her chest, leaving a comfortable hollow, a refreshing coolness around her heart. She would simply camp out in front of the lodger's door and thrust the papers upon him. She cleaned up the living room slowly, one ear trained to the hallway, wondering if he would come out and claim the squalor he had foisted upon them.

Jeisy went to pick up the children with trepidation, worried that he'd wreck everything again, but after she'd fetched them and they'd returned chattering and bright-eyed to the house, she saw that everything was much as she'd left it. That night, she told the children about their father's disappearance, and as she'd expected, the grief was more than what she could bear. They asked the questions she'd asked her husband's boss, and she had no satisfactory answers. While they cried, she sailed away on her own thoughts. It struck her that she had not cried. She couldn't quite make sense of her husband being missing. The problems with the lodger filled her mind. It was far easier to rage at the lodger than to feel her sorrow.

The lawyer faxed the paperwork to her the following day while the children were at school. Each sheet of paper was still hot as she compiled and stapled them together. She signed her name and went to wait in front of the lodger's door. She knocked and when, as usual, he didn't answer, she sat cross-legged in the hall. He'd have to use the bathroom eventually. Hours ticked by until it was time to pick up the children. She squirmed, looking at the watch. Just one more minute. One more.

She gave up and drove to get the children. When they entered the house, she heard the sound of a flushing toilet and ran down the hall. He had already vanished into his room—of course he had.

Jeisy sat down cross-legged again to wait. She asked Antolina to make sandwiches for her siblings for dinner. She sat there after the children had gone to bed. Eventually, sometime after midnight, her eyes closed, and when she woke it was eight in the morning. The eviction notice was still in her hands. There were drops of water on the carpet beside her. And sure enough, the bathroom was full of humid air, the kind of air so thick it seemed to hold memories.

I know you're there! Why are you doing this to us? This is torture, you know? Torture!

She slipped the eviction notice under the door. When she told her attorney, he said that this service might be insufficient, but she tried not to think about that.

On the day of the hearing, the judge dismissed the case when the lodger failed to show up, and she had to admit she hadn't personally served him, that she'd never seen him at all.

I told you as much, the lawyer said. She no longer detected the silk in his voice. Now that her case had proven to be a dud, he was using a rougher voice, brusque, burlap. She paid him with a personal check and returned home weary and exhausted. More pictures had been changed and a new couch sat in the living room, ugly, modern, not at all to her taste.

Her husband's boss phoned again. Another search had been conducted on Petermann Island, but none of the missing people had been found. Rotely, she turned on the TV. Perhaps it didn't matter that the lodger was there, rent-free. He hadn't done anything to *them*. But it irritated her to think of him believing he'd pulled a fast one on her. That because she was alone—a widow, she made herself think—she wouldn't have the gumption to get rid of him.

The following night—or maybe another night after, since there no longer seemed to be markers, dark or light, she could rely upon—after she cooked dinner, she realized with a start the lodger had changed all the dining room furniture. He'd replaced all the chairs.

Every day there was something new. He painted the living room orange. He brought in hideous furniture that collapsed or sat on cinderblocks like a car about to be worked on in the driveway. All the paintings were different yet again. He'd taken away the silk flowers altogether. He replaced the utensils. He replaced her mother's china.

Time rolled on and soon none of the original furnishings remained in the house. One day she came home, and the little yellow house was painted blue. Antolina left for college, and then Noel, and then Aaron. The lodger filed an application with the city to change the number of her house and asked for a zoning variance for the room. The city called her to ask questions and told her that he wanted to build a second story.

But he can't do this, can he? she asked the lawyer.

His voice was full of silk again. It's been a decade, he said. What does that mean?

He's squatted in there so long, he can claim it under the laws of adverse possession. She wrote the lawyer a personal check again, unsure for what, but he seemed to expect it.

Jeisy realized she was on her own: she had to remove the lodger by force. It was the only way. He would never leave on his own. She packed a bag and put it in the car, and then she lit a match in the kitchen. She dropped it on the floor and poured vegetable oil. For a moment, she had doubts. She should grab the baking soda from the refrigerator and put it out. The grease fire spread. It would claim all of the lodger's things, the furniture, the pictures.

On the front lawn, she waited for him to be smoked out.

The house glowed with flames. The house spit flames toward the sky. Dancing orange and gold. Blue-hearted. The walls blackened and crumbled to the ground. The neighbors called the fire department. She stood waiting, not allowing anyone to drag her away. She was determined to see the lodger once and for all now that he'd destroyed everything she could remember of her home. But as the last wall came down, the lodger never emerged.

LITTLE CLAY BOY

THAT WINTER MORNING, BEFORE THE world awoke, Dimitra decided to sculpt the little boy she'd hoped she would one day have with a man she loved. A boy she could sit on the porch with, drinking afternoon tea and talking. She'd long since realized she wouldn't meet either the man or the boy, but the realization never turned into a felt knowledge. She longed for conversations, for a back-and-forth rhythm. Even if only someone who would ask her how her day had been. There was the checkout person at the grocery store asking how she'd been but not wanting the real answer, the mailman saying hello, the woman in charge of the neighborhood brigade requesting her to sign something for the city council. But there was no *talk*, with meaning. At night, she tossed in her fluffy bed with energetic despair, nobody there to witness with her the sharp sound of crickets like ice picks against the night. Perhaps sculpting would be an exorcism, her fingers in clay, working it, sapping her body of energy.

Why this day? Why not? It was a morning like others, blighted by everlasting drought and wildfire smoke. Except this day it came to her that she could make the little boy she wanted, instead of the pots she didn't.

The shingled cottage in back of the house was drafty, densely cold. Dimitra kept an espresso maker on a shelf in the corner and made mugs of burning-hot black espresso, but the caffeine barely affected her. She sculpted in a dream state, her hands guided invisibly. Leaves rustled dark against the dreamy, pinkening sky. Frogs symphonized in the wooden hot tub outside, even though she'd taken care to cover it, and noisy crows gossiped and shrieked among the eucalyptus. Good day, sound-wise, to be born, she thought, taking special care with the shape of the boy's skull, not wanting it to be too smooth. While she understood that phrenology had been discredited, she still preferred the archaic notion that maybe you could tell some things about a person by the bumps on their skull, and she was determined to sculpt a boy everyone would agree was good.

Hour after hour, she slid clay away from his shoulders, between his legs, under his arms, her skin a darker brown than the clay. She ran wet hands over the clay torso, smoothing it and smoothing it, avoiding sudden movements for fear of throwing a nose or an elbow out of joint. His tender lips and dimpled cheeks. Tiny flaring nose and petulant chin. Steady shoulders. He was the size of a six-year-old boy. He emerged from the giant gray block of clay with one foot determinedly ahead of the other, as if he were ready to break into a run and disappear into the gaudy future.

The light was dimming by the time Dimitra finished down to the carefully engraved buttons on his clay shirt and the gentle creases and stitching on his clay jeans. She glanced at the clock and wondered whether there was time to slide him into the kiln but decided against it, lest she make a mistake and cook him too long. But she stood for a long time admiring him, the just-right crook of his elbow, and as she gazed at him, she thought she saw him move his foot a little closer to the other one. She shook her head. It was desire. If only her life had traveled along a different path. He might be real. He might be waking up too early and climbing into bed with her like a heat-seeking missile, eager to talk about his plans for the day. Love for her sculpture flooded her.

The light in the studio was poor, just a light bulb hanging from the ceiling. She tugged on the chain. The studio fell back into its usual gloom. She trudged through the twilight and rosemary back to the main house, feeling a little unsteady, everything gathering under a pleasant blur as her eyesight was no longer as good as it once had been.

After washing her hands, she prepared a modest dinner and then paid her bills. She sat slumped at her dining room table, thinking about her day's work and wondering what had possessed her to sculpt a life-size boy. She'd used almost all her clay reserves to make him. He was equivalent to fifty pots she could have thrown. Relieved she hadn't placed him in the kiln, she wondered whether, come morning, she should pound him back down into a formless slab. People wanted pots, you could do something with pots. There was nothing you could do with a clay boy.

Dimitra woke a few hours later to the sounds of an intruder in the backyard. Rustling near the bushes. The screech of the lawn chair against concrete, a sound so sharp she sat bolt upright in her bed. Through the windows, still nothing but stars. Was it a deer? They'd been wandering into the neighborhoods more often because of the wildfires. She heard it again. Footsteps against the cement. She put on her robe and slippers and tiptoed into the chilly night, nervous, but also protective of her sculpture, unsure what she would do if she found a thief near the shed.

In the shadows, Dimitra glimpsed an even darker figure. She flicked on the porch light. A brown boy grabbing blackberries by the fistful from the bramble along the fence. He didn't seem at all perturbed by the thorns, stuffing the fruit into his mouth. Juice ran down his chin. She stood on the steps and stared at him: the creases in his jeans looked familiar, like ones she had run her hands across. Could it be? She glanced at the door of the shed and saw that it was indeed ajar. Should she speak? Perhaps it was untoward to speak to a blackberry thief, perhaps a line divided the person simply trying to eat and the person who owned a fruit bush, and it was best not crossed, but instead respected. It unnerved her not to go back in and lock the door. But then again, she asked herself, why shouldn't she speak? The longer she looked, the more familiar his features appeared. He was hers, all hers, after all. She'd paid for the clay. She'd worked it.

Are you ... all right? Do you want to come in? Dimitra asked.

He nodded and came right up to her on the porch. He stood before her trembling, on the precipice, perhaps, of living. She wanted to pat his spiky hair down, though she'd sculpted it to stand up a bit. She pulled the screen door open and gestured for him to enter. The floorboards of the old porch whined as he walked across them.

Inside, he sat at the dining room table facing the garden. Dimitra made him pancakes and chocolate milk. He ate with silent ferocity. She asked questions, where had he come from? What did he want? How did he digest his food? But he had no answers. He grunted in order to assent, as well as to demur. When he was finished eating, she showed him the study. You can sleep in here, she said. He nodded.

She placed a sleeping bag on the floor, and then a pillow. He lay down on the bag and stared up at her. It seemed he had something to say but couldn't say it. Or perhaps this was simply the expression she'd sculpted onto his lips and eyebrows.

WANT TO PLAY CATCH? Dimitra asked when they woke at dawn. It seemed like the sort of thing you might ask a boy of this age. He nodded. They went into the garden. She fetched a baseball that the prior owner had left behind in the gardening shed. She showed him how to hold his hand and to cradle his palms to catch the ball. The first and second time, he dropped it and squealed, as if to ask why she was throwing things at him. Take a deep breath, she said. This is just throwing the ball around. My father did it with me, and his father did it with him.

After a few more tries, the boy seemed to breathe easier. They tossed the ball back and forth. She threw gently, almost afraid of hurting him. With practice, he threw with greater force, oblivious to the differences between them.

They spent the morning that way, in an idle paradise. Steady slap of the ball against her palm, and then his, and then hers again. Lunchtime came, and the boy stared at her, big-eyed, again eating with gusto, though who knew where he put it. Dimitra thought she might get some work done, but he stood at the door to the cottage and tapped his foot irritably, and when she didn't respond, he threw himself down on the porch and howled, an emperor. Apparently, she was not to work now that he was here.

They drove northwest to eat oysters and hike with the tule elk. They hiked along what used to be a creek. The clay boy was not to get wet. But there was no need to keep him from going in because it had been cracked and dry for as long as California had been in perilous drought, which was almost Dimitra's whole life. The pair kept a safe distance from the tule elk, but the elk ran east, alarmed by her presence—or equally likely, the clay boy's. He didn't speak, but a quiet understanding grew between them. What she did, he did. He was assimilating to the society of the fleshly.

For months, they seemed to comprise an entire universe unto itself. He played wordless pranks, a hidden whoopee cushion under the down pillows of her bed, a rubber eyeball oozing red plastic in the licorice she stored in the kitchen, and she pretended to be surprised, even overwhelmed. Although he was only a little boy made of clay, his energy was startling. He convinced her to go running in the hills above her house. It was while they were running in the hills that she realized he was a much better runner than she was. Slow down, she panted. I can't keep up.

And he would slow down, but every once in a while speed up, as if it was a joke.

SPRING CAME, AND WITH it, light rains and a yearning for newness. Dimitra heard the clamor of children tromping past the bungalow and down the hill in the mornings, and then back up the hill, in a herd, in the afternoons. She wondered what it would be like for her boy to be with the other children, whether he would start speaking if he were around children of his age. I should enroll you in school, I guess, she said with some trepidation. She didn't want to let him go, but there was a progressive school down the street where they valued social-emotional learning and project-based learning. Parents were required to volunteer so that it felt like a community. This could be good for her little clay boy, and she would be involved too.

She sent him to school with a red lunch box, but at noon, the counselor for at-risk students called her. Your boy doesn't get on with the other children. There was, how do I put this? An incident. At lunchtime. And he hit the other boy back. You should probably pick him up.

Why was there an incident? What did they do to him?

I'm not sure. They say he started it.

Is it because he can't speak? Were they taunting him?

I don't know about that, said the counselor. He can't speak? I thought he was just quiet.

I'll let the principal know, but we'd appreciate it if you'd pick him up.

Dimitra walked to the school. He was lying on the floor of the principal's office and howling as if his heart would break. His eyes were flooded with tears, his nose had been knocked out of joint, so that the nostrils faced a little sideways. She gathered him off the ground and held him in her arms for a few minutes. The principal, who sat in front of a long row of tiny model sports cars and rockets, explained he'd investigated and that one of the boys had beaten him up with his lunch box because he was made of clay.

He was merely curious about his new classmate: there's no blood, of course, he said. There's been no provocation. The other boy said he did it because it was fun to see the clay shift out of place. You can understand that, right? It's weird.

Dimitra shook her head no, feeling trembly. He was in your care, she said tightly, and left in a hurry, unable to hold this sense of confrontation, the reckless urge to shout obscenities at him for being a bigot and on the wrong side.

How are you feeling? she asked him on the long walk uphill on Euclid.

He shook his head and wouldn't say another word. His face was streaming with tears, and he sobbed, wordless. This is it, she thought in a moment of clarity that was soon buried beneath her desire to hear the details of what had happened, language was inadequate, and this was all the talk he needed, and it had to be enough.

She took him home and put a new shirt on him, and carefully pushed his little brown nose back in place. She noticed one of his shoulders had gotten higher than the other in the scuffle, and she carefully pushed it back into place. He looked at her with tears pooled in his big eyes. They don't see you the way I see you, she said, but they will. What she wondered was whether she'd made a mistake in sending him there. But he was alive, wasn't he? Even if made of clay. She hated the kid who'd beaten him up with a passion that unnerved her: people shouldn't feel that strongly about anything. Maybe there was something profoundly wrong with her—the strength of her feelings. She looked up the phone number of the bully's mother to give her a talking-to but began again to doubt her reasons for sending the boy to school at all. Perhaps she should have known, and the decision hinged on her own vanity—or perhaps these were lessons all children learned.

In a few days, the old feelings came back: the desire to talk to him about his day, for him to confide in her. If they spent enough time on it, he could learn, same as anyone else. She began to teach him at home. Letters and numbers. Slowly, slowly, sounds floated from between his lips: *ah* and *ooh* and *oh* and *ah* again. By summer, he was forming whole words, and by winter, stringing together sentences, even if perpetually mixing up his consonants, unable to find his linguistic footing when more than one word was involved.

Dimitra would say a sentence first: The quick brown fox jumped over the lazy dog. And he would reply: The buick qrown fox jumped over the dazy log. She'd repeat and he'd repeat, but there was no forcing his clay tongue to form the sentence properly.

I don't tant to walk! he'd shout. I don't tant!

What are you saying? She'd lose her patience and snap at him, forgetting he was only clay. And then, when she kept trying to quiz him, kept trying to mold him into a child she could take places, he would curl up in a ball and sob. Try as she might, she wouldn't be able to unstick him from himself. His tears ran across his clay nose, which melted into his knee. His elbows oozed into his thighs. His hair tilted forward, cascading onto the floor.

Dimitra would carefully pick him up and try to put him back together, mold him to make the ideal boy, certain that if he had come to life, surely he was also able to be made into the son she'd dreamed of. But as the days stretched on, he more and more frequently collapsed into a fetal position, losing his shape on the tiles of the kitchen floor.

Do you want to try to go back to school? she asked him. Perhaps being around children your age would help you have conversations more easily.

No! I don't sant to go to whool! No whool! No whool.

They play games like red rover and duck, duck, goose, she said, though she wasn't sure these were the enticements she hoped they would be.

No whool! No whool!

Dimitra might have dropped it, but the next month, somebody from the school district called and asked whether she would be enrolling him for the coming year. Or are you homeschooling? the woman on the phone asked after Dimitra mumbled something akin to a no.

I was homeschooling him, but it hasn't taken.

She had mostly given up on language, his clay tongue a Rubicon. She was mortified trying to think of why the woman from the school district would have singled her out, and simultaneously, she secretly wished that her son could try to be one of the kids at school, growing up the way she'd grown up, the way she'd imagined. Did somebody complain about us?

No, no. The principal you spoke to left the school because his values did not mesh with ours, and we are trying to fix any problems with the files he handled.

Do we need to come back? she asked, weighing her fear of another incident against her desperate, half-buried hope he'd have the experiences of ordinary children.

You don't have to, of course, but we think it would be a good idea, the woman said.

She tried to ready the little clay boy, tried to familiarize him with the notion of going back to school. She blew through a hundred stories about first days of school. She packed his schoolbag with books and a stuffed whale. She reminded him that before the incident with his lunch, he'd been jumping around with excitement over school.

No whool! he cried as she buttoned his shirt the next morning, tears running over his little clay nose and dripping onto the wooden floorboards. No whool!

She dragged him out of the house, careful not to pull too hard on his arm, and they began the walk through the hilly streets toward the school. She tried not to pull too hard on his arm for fear of pulling it clean off. When the school building came into view, he pulled loose of her. You can't match kee! You can't match kee! he shouted, running, his backpack bouncing against his back. She ran after him, fury mounting in her chest. Full of determination not to do what she wanted him to do, he ran so hard and so fast up the hill that she couldn't keep up. Can't match kee! Can't match kee! Because of its nonsensical structure, his taunt was unable to wound her, but she couldn't laugh with her heart pounding as it was. He dropped his backpack and when she slowed to pick it up, he broke into an even faster sprint. Though she tried to follow, he ran farther and farther away, a little dark figure under the leafy trees.

She stopped and flopped onto the ground, air tearing through her lungs. At first, she thought it was her tears dribbling onto her legs, and then she realized it was raining. Large drops of rain. She looked up. In the distance, the little boy stood in the heavy rain. His head tilted back as he looked up at the raging storm coming for him with the anticipation of a lover hoping to water all of the dead things. Or the things that had never lived at all.

Even as she approached him, she could see it was too late.

Water ran down his body, gathering clay as it rolled to his feet. Bood-gye, he said. Bood-gye.

I'll put you back together, she insisted.

His head disappeared into the wet first, then his shoulders drooped. In moments, he gathered himself into a fetal position on the sidewalk, and the clay that had once been his elbows, his knees, ran along the sloped concrete in rivulets, disappearing into the reflections of cedars in the puddles.

THE NIGHT THE
MOVERS CAME

ANOTHER FAMILY IS MOVING INTO the peach-colored Victorian opposite ours off Main Street. Dawn ushers in four burly and tattooed movers who are whistling with their sensuous lips, who flash their big vicious white teeth to anyone they see in a kind of fear grimace, and who begin hauling leather couches and an armoire and glass tables and plush overstuffed armchairs through the green front door, which is a copy of ours, into the inky vacancy beyond. The movers are yapping. Loud enough to hear, even from bed, but not so loud I can understand. They are all moving in slow motion, limbs oozing in and out of the other house's door—the movers and the family—as if I were pushing a button to change their speeds, like I could halt the earth's tilt and start it up before moving it another direction again.

I look out the window through the long lace. Even though they seem liquid and relaxed as they travel, the movers do not take a minute to wipe their shoes before crossing the wooden bumper at the threshold. I imagine their big feet tracking dirt through the parlor. Big muddy footprints as they tromp up the stairs and into the mauve master bedroom, a mirror of my

own bedroom, where I am waiting for my husband K and our
son to return from sailing, with stories of gray whale sightings,
moments when a soft haze floats right above the waves and a
migrating whale comes up to the surface blowing water, its tail
lifting gracefully before it submerges. Five minutes pass before
it needs to come up again, my son always points out.

It is a terrible week to move into our neighborhood. We
used to be a lemonade-and-cookies place, a leave-your-door-
unlocked paradise. Toddlers drawing seascapes with chalk and
riding shiny red tricycles. Barbeques in each backyard. The
tranquil slip of the Pacific that lies downhill from our houses
visible behind two palms, foreign transplants that have been
icons for as long as I can remember.

But last week a man was tied to his chair during a home
invasion robbery in the house across the way, a house built at
the end of the century before last, same as ours. He described
the robbers as Pac-Men moving swiftly and quietly through
the rooms, gobbling his possessions. I can't stop thinking about
those Pac-Men inching forward, their mouths swallowing the
love seat and the walnut-and-burl chairs.

I leave my post at the second-floor bedroom window. In
the adjoining bathroom, I force the spearmint toothpaste from
a tube with dwindling supply and run the toothbrush across
my teeth in a back-and-forth, relentless metronome. First the
front two teeth—get them bright and shiny—then the left
side of my mouth, then the right. Spit a mouthful of froth into
the pink porcelain sink. Froth, spit. In the mirror, I bare my
teeth and run a finger over my canines.

I try to picture what those robbers might have looked like,
but the father across the street did not have a strong descrip-
tion to share with me or the police. Or maybe he didn't want
to talk about it. After a moment, I seem to move through a

telescope and realize that all of this was a long time ago, but then I telescope back again.

It is not as if I have anything of value for the robbers to take. Not anymore. I'm by myself now. I set my toothbrush down next to the sink, feeling a wave of dizziness as I always do when I look at the tiny black-and-white tiles on the floor.

Inside the bedroom, against the wall, a black-and-white movie flickers and hums like an old-school film projector. *Tick-tick-tick*, the reel unwinding. Three-two-one, the numbers count down on the screen. I don't know where the projector is, but after I search for a little bit to find the source of the light, I give up and sit down on the edge of the bed and stare. On the wall, the tooth travels up an angular black channel like an off-white Pac-Man, or perhaps more like the dots a larger circle eats. The tooth is wandering through a floor plan, and every time he passes a piece of furniture it disappears, and the tooth bumps along, like he has someplace to go. I realize, after a moment, the floor plan is the same as my house's floor plan. There's the parlor, the sitting room, the curving staircase, the hall with three bedrooms coming off of it. He is eating my furniture.

The quiver of the tooth is what gets me. I want to straighten it, put it in its proper place. It is challenging me: *You feel stable? You feel stable? You shouldn't feel stable.* Again, the feeling of rising into the air, a crystalline clarity: K is not coming back with our son. Terror overwhelms me again; perhaps I've dreamed them up. But no, surely not, there was K last night, scrubbing dishes so he and our son could go out on the water early. I did not see him this morning, and there was no dent on the side of the bed. Perhaps the movers woke them while I was still sleeping. I surface for a moment into this realization, but then I'm returned to my body, and run a finger against my canines and wonder if I'm right that they've gotten longer and sharper.

I could watch the movie all night.

I have not been on my medication for a while, I realize, but there was nothing manic about the way I brushed my teeth. Nothing sped up—or slowed down even, but there were those neighbors oozing in and out of doors, lento, like ice cream drizzling down the side of a cone, before switching to a bright allegro. I remember with a start that the parlor used to have a piano. I think it was stolen. K played piano. If he were home he could measure my speed while brushing, and perhaps even my speed while thinking, by which I really mean the speed of my talking, of course.

That tooth is still moving up the wall, through that projected floor plan, and it seems that even though the tooth keeps eating furniture and technically it should be gone by now, there is always more furniture for the tooth to eat. I wonder again where the movie is coming from, where the source is. I examine the space behind the bedside table and ensure there are no openings in the wall that divides the bathroom and bedroom from which light might be projected. No suspicious cords or boxes I don't recognize. No robber hiding there either; I make sure to check. I yank the down comforter aside and search under the bed again for a projector. Nothing there, nothing there. There is no source evidently. The autumn wind howls dry and ominous, a wind shot through with yellow-brown deciduous leaves and bonfire smoke and prickly sweet gum seeds. A wind that intimates wolves, a wind that brings the scent of lemons and oranges and roses from the gardens around the block. I trudge down the hall to close my son's bedroom window. I don't bother to flick on the light switch, I just want to guard myself against that wretched howl, which is so lonely and dark it echoes in my bones.

Moving the bed a little to the side, I scan the baseboard of the wall opposite the film, and the windows of the neighboring houses and the street. I search inside the window seat. No projector. No wires. No listening devices. Nothing, nada, zip. Whoever is screening this film must have hidden everything well.

The tooth blinks on the wall, like a cursor on a screen. It blinks and blinks, and there is nothing to show for all that except the floor plan, all those empty rooms. I don't know what the significance of that floor plan is, what could that filmmaker have been thinking?

Downstairs there are footsteps, firm, that creak against the floorboards. I shove the nightstand out of the way, open the bedroom door, and peer over the white rail of the landing down to the hardwood floor below. Two moving men are carrying the couch out of my living room, down the hall past the staircase, and through the front door.

You don't need to take that, I call to them.

The one with big teeth looks up absently but doesn't seem to hear. I run back to the bedroom window. The moving men are carrying my furniture across the street and into the neighbor's condo across the court. They disappear inside, and then return to take the armchairs and tables.

I search for my shoes and clothes, but can't find them, so I run downstairs barefoot, wearing only my robe. I make a mental inventory of what's missing before checking the backyard. A long, aggressive passionflower vine curls through the glossy leaves of the lemon trees, strangling them. Strung along the vine, like musical notes, are flowers with baroque purple centers and thin creamy petals. Hundreds of lemons are bloated and overripe, and have fallen to the ground, splatted against the concrete patio, and gone to mold. I should have picked them earlier, I suppose. I have a vague recollection of making lemon pickle. Jars and jars of it. The citrus trees were overproducing. K eventually lost his temper about the mess I made in the kitchen. The heady fragrance of the lemons filling our house. My hands bloody from the thorns and stinging, stinging with the lemon juice in my wounds. There's so much I don't remember, deep cavities in my memory. I should weed. K will be so upset that I've let the plot go like that.

I slide the door shut and hurry into the living room. A moving man hefts a chair above his head and clunks through the front door into the smoky dusk. I run after him, shouting, Wait, wait! The black asphalt is cool and smooth beneath my bare feet.

A Vietnamese neighbor in a pink sweater, who I almost recognize, approaches and grabs me by the arm before I can reach the moving man. She seems to think she knows me. How are you today, Mrs. Amrita? Everything all right?

Of course. Everything's fine, I say. I pull my dressing gown tight around my stomach and draw myself up.

I haven't seen you in a couple of weeks, Amrita. How are you keeping busy in there? She gestures at my house.

I smile to be polite. This woman is very forward, but she probably doesn't intend me any harm. Oh, you know, watching my reality programs, waiting for K and the baby to get back from their trip.

The woman looks taken aback, and then her eyes go dark and her face twists a little as if she's pained by my words. She asks slowly, a little condescendingly, Do you need me to call your son and have him come by to check on you again?

Who does she think she is? How would a baby check on me? Something must be wrong with her.

No, thank you, I say, pulling my dressing gown more tightly around myself and trying not to show that she makes me nervous.

K will bring my little boy home. He took the car seat, I say. I tap my foot impatiently against the ground. All my neighbors' cars are in their driveways or parked in front of their houses, but it disturbs me that I don't recognize these cars— are all my neighbors new?

She nods vigorously. Uh, huh, I'm sure he will, but just to make sure, let me give your son a call . . .

I sigh. Have you met any of these new neighbors yet?

The woman looks puzzled. Nobody new has moved onto our street for years.

Fed up with the woman's total lack of knowledge about anything worth knowing, I decide to go back inside and come out later, when I'm sure she's inside her own house where she belongs. You're of no use to me, I announce.

I'll bring some flowers over later, she says, as if we know each other well.

Inside the hallway, however, more is missing. The statute of Saraswathi, goddess of knowledge, is gone. So are the framed black-and-white photographs, even the ones of the baby. The lithographs with witty storks staring down at a snail. Gone. The antique love seat with velvet upholstery. Disappeared.

A frantic sound—my heart quickening. I must check upstairs.

Once I turn on the light, my son's room looks forlorn without the toddler bed, without the stacks of Amar Chitra Katha comic books, without the toys he will play with for years to come. What kind of robbers are these? They have taken a toddler bed. They have even taken his clothes from the dresser drawers!

My teeth are badly in need of brushing again. Furry. It's like weeks have passed since I last brushed them, though I thought I'd started just before the furniture began vanishing this morning.

I walk slowly through our master bedroom into the bathroom and take my toothbrush from beside the sink and try to do the morning over again. I am still brushing when the telephone on the nightstand rings. With my mouth still full of spearmint foam, I greet the person on the other end of the line.

Mom, is that you? the voice says, an adult American man's voice. Young, maybe college-age.

Who's this? I ask, after swallowing the foam.

Someone sighs and clears his throat on the other end. It's Sachin. Your son, Mom.

What? My own son still calls me mommy! I am trying to remain pleasant, even though the man sounds slightly hostile, and even though a horrible chill comes over me and my arms have gone all bumpy—somebody is trying to trick me. Probably some college kid, home for break, one too many beers. Who is this? This is not funny.

It's me. It's fucking me, he says louder. I sense a keening desperation in his voice, but I don't know how to help. He says, in a resigned voice, I can't do this anymore. I can't take it. I don't think Mrs. Pham can take this either, always sending you back inside the house.

I don't answer. I hear him tapping a cord against wood. Maybe he's talking from a landline.

Are you watching that old movie Dad made, the one that makes you happy?

How does he know about this, the modern riff on the Méliès films that my husband never showed anyone but me, a movie he failed to get optioned by a studio?

You know, something is on, I say carefully. But I can't find the projector.

He sighs again. Not this again. We need to get you a live-in caregiver. We love Mrs. Pham, we can't put her through this.

How does he know Mrs. Pham? Regardless, I don't want strangers in my home, taking up space, misusing the early nineteenth-century oven, leaving the shower running, complaining about the lack of electricity at the receptacles. I like to wander around my house, play with my son, and keep up with the latest science journals, though there is nobody with whom to share the Salk Institute's discoveries. I used to work there once, I remind myself. Of course, like all the young people these days, this young man is trying to sell me something, a different reality. I hear the *shur-shur* of footsteps moving around downstairs on the Kashani carpet. What are they taking now?

Listen, can't really talk right now, sir, I tell the person on the other end.

What are you doing? Never mind, stay put, I'm coming.

That's not necessary. I hang up. Now the old staircase is creaking with footfalls. I open the bedroom door and walk down the hall. Three unsmiling movers from across the street are stepping up to the landing in a row, smelling of grass and dirt, their teeth too bright up close. They march into my room. They look vaguely familiar, the contours of their faces like some dream I've dreamed before but forgotten when the morning light hit my face. They don't seem to notice the movie on the wall.

Two lift the mattress from the bed frame and the other grabs the nightstand. They bump the furniture against the stucco wall in the stairwell. Careful, careful, I call after them, confused. Do I know these men? Are they robbers? The same ones who hurt the man across the street? Or are we moving? K didn't say anything about it.

As they haul the furniture across the court, I see the small boy riding his shiny red tricycle around the court in the dark. My son's old tricycle. I recognize the large reflectors I had fitted to it.

I open my window and call down through the screen. Are your parents inside? Are you using my son's tricycle? He doesn't even look up. It's as if I haven't spoken. He zooms around under the streetlamp, making figure eights. A few minutes later, the movers clunk back up the stairs in their big boots. They've come for the tarnished gold bed frame, my lovely bed frame with crystal orb bedknobs.

I scream, What are you doing? And when they don't respond, I try a different tack. Can't you see that tooth on the wall? It might be eating furniture now, but I can promise you it's coming for you next.

They ignore me.

Watching them enter the other house yet again with my furniture, I realize that the boy and his tricycle are gone. I miss my son and my husband with a strange and total longing, but the Pac-Man movie keeps playing, relentless, consuming everything familiar.

The lights of the house across the way are on. The lower level glows softly, as if a flashlight is being shone through wax paper in the windows. The family is eating rice pilaf and dosai at a small breakfast table—my breakfast table, I note with a start of recognition. The movers have given my furniture to this family. But I do not begrudge them the things they have stolen. They are just starting out.

When we moved in a few years ago, how happy, how *euphoric* we were. A shimmering warmth vibrated around our hearts.

A fort of brown cardboard boxes, presumably filled with kitchenware, looms behind the other three at the table. The toddler zooms between rooms, back and forth, not unlike the Pac-Man. In a few days, my K will be home with our boy, and we will walk over to meet the new little neighbor under the pretense of asking if they have some sugar we could borrow for the dessert we're making, and we will lift the brass-plated knocker on the door and tap it three times like we're in a fairy tale about bears and princes. We will chalk seascapes on the asphalt and time tricycle races. As the years pass, the boy and our son will become fast friends. I will have another mother with whom to drink blue tea and play old records. Our husbands will play pickleball together at the tennis courts; that's what people do now, right? Play pickleball? It sounds like code for something corny and sexual, so I try not to think about it.

That tooth keeps on bumping through the maze. What a dogged little tooth to keep going in the face of all those corners, no endpoint in sight. Later, Mrs. Pham will come back with the flowers, but for now, I sit cross-legged on the rug in my empty room and watch, and watch, and watch the bright tooth chipping away at the night, a soft warmth in my chest like a sunrise, the light that allows the tooth to continue his passage through the warren of hallways coming from somewhere I cannot see.

THE FOG CATCHERS

ON ONE OF THE LAST entirely unprotected beaches left on the Central Coast, a group of fishermen stand at the edge of the vast gray waves, swearing obscenities at the fish who are not biting. Viduna sips from a box of water the concierge gave her and reads from a Henry Miller novel, looking up occasionally at the dark silhouettes of the fishermen, at the dark gray rocks she'd called hieroglyphic rocks when she was little, rocks embedded with sharp white shells, swirls of white. Every once in a while, she catalogs the hotel guests she saw at breakfast, at the Inn's stargazing hour the night before. Occasionally, they wander by, holding hands. All couples, none likely to part with their money. At a resort in Gold Beach, a month earlier, she'd met a mark right away. An elderly white financier, eager to have his ego stroked, eager to believe her—this was not unusual. The funds she talked him out of are financing her stay in the Inn.

The summer sun is a red-hot blaze above all the gray by the time she's ready to leave. She trudges back barefoot across the sand stained with purple to the parking lot. Beside the car, a band of fog catchers waits, holding large glass bottles full of white swirling fog. She could swear she saw them on the coast in Oregon too.

You're here by the ocean again, the woman says, her voice tense, questioning, knowing. How was it last night? she asks.

How was what? Viduna asks, confused.

You know! The man with the little brown braids sneers. What he's insinuating isn't clear.

I don't, she says, unsure whether to unlock her door, unsure why they're following her. Are they onto her? Are they working for the dysfunctional government? Dysfunction or not, they seem too much misfits to be informants of any kind.

We see what you're reading, another of the men says, as if this is an explanation. His bottle of fog is large, and he clutches it with both hands.

She unlocks her door and slips into the car hurriedly, trying not to show that a thick dread has flooded her; her throat seems to close as she thinks about speaking to them. She locks the door after she slams it shut. The fog catchers remain where they are, still talking, watching as she pulls out of her spot and drives onto the bumpy narrow road that leads back to Highway 1. Back to the Inn. The man with the little brown braids seems to be laughing in the rearview mirror as she peels away. She looks at the road ahead and refuses to think further about the fog catchers, about the nagging intuition that they are following her, and focuses her attention where it needs to be: making money. She may not have found the right mark last night or this morning amid the throngs of wealthy, older people, but that doesn't mean there won't be someone at the restaurant tonight. It can take time to pull off a heist, and she has nothing but time.

AFTER SUNSET, VIDUNA SCARFS down her dinner, all four courses. The last, a sumptuous slice of dark chocolate cake with pink sea salt, she washes down with a glass of sparkling rosé, its bubbles flying down her throat, liquid divinity. Outside the enormous window, fog rolls in along the cliffside.

The band of fog catchers troop into the restaurant, raucous. They're dingy from trekking the Pacific Coast Highway, across the property to this restaurant on the cliff, and she wonders if they have money to buy dinner. Judging by the rags they're wearing, their filthy, frayed jeans and grimy faces, they don't. They set large jars of fog, swirling a lamplit white behind glass, on the round table. How did they get past the security guard at the property's entrance? They must have hiked in from one of the trails through the forest.

Just look at our haul, one says to the other, proudly tossing those little brown braids off his back.

Beautiful, man.

The waiter brings a decanter of wine, carefully pouring each a taste.

We'll get so much for them, says the woman. She takes a big sip, finishing off the taste of red wine.

We're gonna make bank, agrees Little Brown Braids.

Everyone at the table laughs, and they continue to drink their house wine.

Viduna tries not to laugh. Where the fuck are they going to sell those bottles of fog? She imagines a swap meet in a parking lot somewhere. Setting those jars on the folding tables in rows. Weak sunlight. Slinking away, grubby pockets heavy with spare change they've traded their bottles for. Not like scamming the wealthy is any better. At least there's a real pay-off when she does it well.

The first time, she hadn't intended the result. At a resort in Vegas, she befriended a frail, sickly man, once a music producer, cracking jokes with him and listening to his stories about Frank Sinatra and Count Basie, the glamorous nights at the club, the beautiful styling on a tenor sax. No sex, just friendship. She discovered not long after, he named her the beneficiary of his retirement account and left her his vacation home in the desert, which she sold. He'd genuinely liked *her*, not whatever ideas she evoked for him, nor because, in cruder terms, she was exotic.

Or has time—twelve years—obscured what truly happened? She can never be sure.

She leans back in the plush seat and takes the last bite of her chocolate cake, closing her eyes at the taste of sea against the sweetness. The suave man at the table next to her turns in his seat and looks at her. She glances at his watch, so often a tell, if not of money, of narcissism. At least five hundred, but his clothes aren't tailored. They bunch in odd places, off the rack. She sets her fork down. The waiter finishes pouring his wine and recedes.

What did you have for dessert? the man asks. He has a moderate, pragmatic tone to his voice.

After she answers, he pauses and screws up his face, like he's thinking, but then asks with a note of brightness in his voice, as if it's somehow an original question, Was the cake good?

Yes, it had the taste of the sea in it. She's expecting this poetic flourish to send him away, confounded. But he continues to look at her as if he wants to be inside her, and so she keeps looking back as a dare.

What else did you have?

She smiles, puzzled at the attempt to make inroads, but he's handsome with intelligent, curious eyes, the gentle lilt of a Persian accent.

Let's see, a hamachi crudo to start, oysters with rosé mignonette, the shrimp and creamy polenta. All of it was delicious, the shrimp especially. What did you order?

The rib eye. If I'd met you a few minutes sooner, maybe I would have ordered the shrimp.

You can't go wrong here, she says. Isn't this place beautiful?

It is. I've never been here. I arrived only a few hours ago. What brings you here?

Passing through, Viduna says.

Going to Los Angeles to be an actress?

She hesitates. Wonders whether he's joking, how he knows acting is her dream when they are so far up north on the coast. She feels what she's felt all this time along the ocean on Highway 1, that she's under surveillance, that there's a force larger than her aware of her every move. Onto her grift.

Yes, I mean, is that cliché? Young woman, alone, on her way to be an actress.

The table of fog catchers has ceased its chatter. Their silence. Viduna glances behind her. The woman fog catcher slides her jar of fog back and forth between her hands with a certain quiet intensity. None openly stare at Viduna, but Little Brown Braids catches her eye. He smiles, as an afterthought, before looking away. They might be laughing to themselves.

No, I guessed that because you're beautiful. Have you been in anything I might have seen?

I was once in a daytime commercial, but I don't know if you would've seen it. For soap.

The man shakes his head. I don't think so.

What do you do? Are you a businessman on a business trip?

He laughs. Businessman! Who asks that? This question gives you away as an actress. No, I'm a lighting designer. I advise politicians on building and lighting seawalls to avoid wrecks and deaths. I don't know that seawalls were the right solution at all, to be honest; there's been a loss of marine wildlife in the intertidal zones. But someone had to step up to make them safer for property owners.

Sounds like a cool job.

She tries to sound convincing. How is this anyone's job? And though she won't admit it to him, what is a C-wall, anyway? It sounds unbearably abstract. She doesn't want to ask and sound disrespectful, but laughs at her own thoughts, and then fears her unexplained laughter makes her sound insincere. The fog catchers speak to each other in soft voices now, and she can't quite catch what they're saying.

He says his name is Dariush. I drove up from L.A. On my way to San Francisco.

That's where I live! Or where I used to live, anyway, she says, and sips her rosé nervously.

Oh, I see! So it's fate for us to have met here in the middle, right? Do you have everything set up in Los Angeles? A job?

I have an apartment in Topanga, and I'll be doing my day job too.

And that is?

She thinks of how to couch her work to make it sound respectable rather than sordid. I guess you could say I'm kind of a real estate agent. But that's not my real calling or anything, just what I do to pay bills.

Do you talk to your real estate clients about these hazards of buying property on the coast?

She shrugs. The heart wants coastal property, I guess.

The waiter arrives with the plate of rare steak, blood oozing from the purpling flesh, some sort of deep-fried tempura green beans and potatoes on the side. Heart attack food. Surprising, since he's so fit, his shoulders squared, boxy, his face clean-shaven, flecks of silver at his temples. A silver fox, that's what they call this kind of man.

Do you want to join me? he asks.

She studies his face. Friendly enough, what's the harm? She stands to go over to his table, and the waiter, turning from replenishing his bread, stands blocking her way and looks at her as if he's expecting a question.

Can I go by you?

She's joining me, Dariush explains.

Oh, I'm sorry! The waiter has a different expression she can't read. She's not sure if it's horror or surprise. She sits at the table with a little irritated sigh.

The fog catchers fall silent again. They are, indeed, watching Dariush and her, with amused, slightly disgusted expressions.

Can I buy you a drink? he asks politely. She declines.

They speak of her acting dreams, they speak of his lighting work. He wanted to be an architect, but his father ran a furniture store and expected him to join him in that line of work as the business expanded, and so he'd wound up a lighting designer for furniture shows before discovering the change you could effect by partnering with local governments on their seawalls.

It all sounds like nonsense, but he reaches out and squeezes her arm, as if to reinforce an emotional skein being woven between them, and it's a kind of electricity, the press of a pedal. He is doing the weaving, or is he Rumpelstiltskin? She wonders how many women he has done this with, even though it hardly seems to matter, because he's so profoundly focused on her face. She's wearing crimson lipstick partly because she was expecting to be alone and wanted to feel less lonely in her aloneness, but soon he's staring at her mouth, a laser focus that makes her lick her lips, unsettled. The intensity of his focus, as if he has a plan for her, unnerves her.

He asks what school she went to before selling real estate, and when she responds, he tells her of how his sisters' children went there, changing into different people, who sternly lectured him about how he spent his money, telling him not to buy property in certain neighborhoods because it drove poor people out—

Gentrification.

What? Yes, that's what they called it. I didn't understand it, this lunacy! That's not what our people are like. We value real estate. If you have the money, you should invest it in property. It's safer to own property. Gentrification, what's that? It's just some people moving to another place, same as all through history. I mean, I do feel sorry for the poor people but—

But you feel you should be free to buy where you want?

He looks relieved to think she's not *that* type of liberal, even though she was merely stating what she could observe about him, watching him scarf down the steak and fried vegetables, the confidence with which he reaches over to squeeze any part of her flesh that shows. Her hand, her knee, her shin crossed over her knee. She knows, of course she knows. But he assumes they are on the same page about this issue, gentrification.

Exactly! I mean, you know, these American citizens, they don't realize how good they have it. You know? You and I, we're different. We're like each other, he says. Again, he tries to build up their relationship.

His brazen effort to make more of the situation than it is, to con her into attraction! She institutes a difference between them, Oh, I'm a citizen. You're . . . ?

No, no, I did become a citizen. He looks taken aback, like he's suddenly afraid she's a xenophobe, in spite of her brown skin. She feels guilty and smiles, trying to show she's just curious, not a scary nativist. The muscles in his face relax. The fog catchers have resumed talking, and it's hard not to eavesdrop.

He continues. But I was twelve when I came here, and it was hard, leaving our home. We were alone here, you know?

Most of the world, like ninety-nine-point-nine percent of the world, doesn't have a chance to figure out who they can be.

We're very lucky, she finishes for him.

She immediately feels for him. Maybe this tack, showing her how similar they are, is working on her, even though her purpose for being here is to find a mark, not engage in flirtation with someone whose financial condition is not at all clear. But he's right, it was hard. She'd come when she was five, and she remembers walking too long with her parents to get anywhere so they could save on the bus fare, how her legs ached, but her parents kept repeating, just a little longer, just a little longer, then finally getting fed up with her whining and shouting at her, so that she quickly realized she should stop saying how she felt about anything, knowing she had no say in what happened in the end anyhow. The paruppu sadam they ate every night because it was cheaper than everything else. Fights about how much her mother had spent on a tin pan to thalichify vegetables. Her mother had spent a quarter: her father thought she should have gone to another store to spend only a nickel.

Before she has a chance to feel too bad for him, however, he reaches over and squeezes her leg, as if to make sure she knows they are the same, which in fact, she already knows, looking into his eyes. They are both looking for someone to convince, but she doesn't like to be reminded so blatantly with intrusions into her space. They're both immigrants, emotionally battered by their childhoods, keen on persuading others to trust them. But what does that matter here in this fancy restaurant? It's difference that makes you lust after someone, why doesn't he know that? Their similarity doesn't bond them, it makes them more likely to despise each other.

She smiles at him anyway. She's used to being misunderstood. She's used to accommodating, if for no reason other than that she doesn't give a shit about courtship and gentleness advances her grift.

Can I get you a glass of something? he asks again.

Okay.

He signals the waiter. Finally, her disdain lifts; there's something in his demeanor, a forcefulness, she finds sexy. She imagines herself against the restaurant wall, him thrusting into her. She squirms in her chair. He looks at her mouth when he's not trying to find some common ground, and that ever-so-tacit acknowledgment of difference, that her body is separate from his, makes her head spin.

She asks the waiter for another rosé, and the waiter is looking at her, questioningly, as if she's crazy, but also in a gentle way. It's as if he knows what is happening better than she does, and whether or not he thought better of her, he sympathizes, though, of course, he will gossip cynically about it later with the waitstaff as they drink their Fernet after hours in the kitchen.

Dariush is telling her about his sisters, who live near him. He always looks out for them, and worries about them; they got to be what they wanted to be, but he was a boy, so he was stuck doing what his father wanted him to do. She nods along, swallowing her impatience.

Do you have sisters or brothers? he asks her.

She shrugs. A sister, I guess.

You don't know?

No, I know. She doesn't want to talk about her older sister, about how her older sister ran away from home when she was a teenager, never to be heard from again; how she thinks about her sister all the time, wondering what happened to her, wondering if someday she'll get a phone call that her sister is dead, a phone call asking her to come identify the body in the morgue.

The waiter brings a glass of rosé. She sips as Dariush continues telling his life story.

I have to use the restroom, she says. She has to escape from Dariush's sincere brown eyes, not quite knowing what to do with herself under an honest gaze of desire. She wraps herself more tightly in her gold cardigan and flees to the bathroom. Inside the restroom, after, when she is washing her hands, the female fog catcher emerges from a stall, and taking a spot beside her at the sink to wash her hands, too, smiles with a disturbing look of knowingness and winks. He's hot, isn't he? the fog catcher asks.

Uneasy, she returns to the table.

Dariush has finished his rib eye and the waiter is at the table, taking away the plate. She sips her rosé again, despite feeling queasy. The rosé makes it worse. A stray thought passes through her mind: has he drugged her drink while she was in the restroom? The woman in the bathroom, her wink? Are the fog catchers in conspiracy with Dariush? She thinks of her run-ins with them along the coast. Maybe the feds *are* onto her, she worries. Sometimes she can't believe how long she's been in this line of work without getting caught. He reaches out and touches her hand. Are you okay?

His solicitousness now makes her nauseous. This is how murders happen. Someone sitting in a bar gets roofied. This is not desire, but a precursor to rape. Something in her body shifts. Or is she imagining he wants to do her harm because she initially thought of him as her mark?

What room are you in? he asks.

She shrugs, every muscle in the back of her neck tensing. Oh, I don't know, I don't remember the name.

Is it oceanside?

Yes, but I mean it's not one of the luxurious ones. It's not right on the coast—

He interrupts, I bet my room is nicer than your room. He says it without the slightest bit of humility, where if she'd made this same statement, she would have immediately qualified it. It reminds her of men she grew up with: even as boys they never felt any need to put themselves down, and she knew, always, she was supposed to put herself down, to appear less threatening than she was, and when she fulfilled their expectations, they immediately liked her more. It was always choosing between being liked and being right, and eventually, she picked being liked—being wrong. She looks at him keenly. She sips her rosé in order not to rouse his suspicion about her suspicion, and because he's calling forth a difference between them, he's attractive again, in a dangerous way. She glances around the restaurant, reminding herself that she's supposed to be looking for someone fantastically wealthy. Dariush is small fry.

I have a film producer friend, he says, dangling it in front of her like live bait. She knows she is supposed to bite, but she doesn't imagine any sort of future timeline in which they know each other. He says, We play poker together. In fact, we were supposed to play poker together tonight.

Instead, you threw caution to the wind and decided to take a road trip?

Yeah, I didn't tell them, my poker buddies. I just needed to get on the road. I needed to take those curves on the 1 north as fast as I could. I didn't even have a reservation here, but I stopped. They had a room.

Sounds dangerous.

This impulsivity, evidently meant to fuel desire, reminds her of herself. Again, she loses interest. She feels flat, bored. She's dying to leave. She will not find a mark at this Inn, yet she simultaneously fears and pities and still faintly desires this man.

She imagines him raping her if he realizes she doesn't want to go through with it. Standing there at the door to her room, with the Do Not Disturb sign hung on the door handle, him pushing her inside, throwing her on the bed.

It was living, man! he says happily, and slaps the table with his palm. Anyway, this is our story, this is how we met in the middle. It feels like something.

She nods. He's either falling for her, which is laughable, or wants her to think he is, wants her to believe there's something more special here than there is. He has a sparkling sincerity, and she cannot pinpoint what it is, old world charm, or a ridiculous player mentality that you need to court a woman with soulmate-talk in order to talk her into fucking you. The assumption being women can't feel desire without persuasion. There is something boyish in his expression, in his desire to be desired for his manly recklessness on the road, and she wants to pat him on the head and tell him good boy.

Coincidence, she says, waving her hand. She can feel the fog catchers' interest, the expectation a grand drama is unfolding before them. She catches the waiter's eye. He comes to the table and asks if he can get them anything else.

Dariush says no, and the waiter leaves.

Well, we're here now, and you're beautiful and this—he gestures grandly at the night sky through the window, the stars breathing. I think we've met because we have to teach each other something.

We're just having a conversation, she says. She speaks firmly, with purpose, so he knows she has lost interest in fucking him, but she can feel her own anxiety in her words, a nebulous thing born of thinking about sex with this stranger she's known at most an hour creeping through.

He sets a small white tube of indica on the table. Here's what I can teach you, he says.

She smiles to be nice, still persisting in social niceties, though the thought of getting high with him, the thought of losing control when she is supposed to be orchestrating trust, alarms her. Her fear might be an intuition that he's already slipped something into her rosé. It tastes strange, she thinks again. He said politicians, but is he undercover with the feds perhaps? Fear rises in her chest. So many ways things can go awry. She moves the glass away from her on the table and looks around the room. Every man who could have been her mark is coupled up. Before her is the only single man, the only viable catch.

You know, I should get going, she says.

Are you sure? What's wrong? He touches her leg on bare skin above her knee again, not aggressively, but suggestively.

Nothing's wrong, I just have to get up early to get back on the road.

Should we breakfast together? His voice is gentle, and she immediately wonders what's making her so anxious. There's nothing about him to suggest he's with the feds. She observes him observing her, baffled by her unwillingness to keep traveling down that road, determined to keep talking about what interests him, childhood.

Fearing she's been contaminated by the rosé, fearing she's been contaminated somehow by the intimacy of this encounter, the way he kept touching her, she jumps up quickly. No, no, but maybe I'll see you around.

He says nothing. The fog catchers fall silent as she hurries past them into the night.

As she returns to the Tree House, she keeps glancing behind her, fearing he'll follow her, but she reaches her room without incident. She digs around her purse, and he doesn't pop out to kill her. She unlocks the door and makes it inside safely, and lights a tiny cup of wax in the fireplace, shifting the logs to make sure the wood catches on the flame. Fear and desire are confusing, the difference between them unclear.

LATE THAT NIGHT, LONG after the fire has gone out, she walks by the fence that crawls with pale-pink star jasmine. Perched on a high cliff blanketed in lavender, the heated basking pool is shaped like a widened horseshoe, surrounded on its curved side by pavers and on the other an infinity edge that appears to drop you into the clouds. Steam, fog, clouds—nearly indistinguishable. She'd been at the pool the night before, the Henry Miller novel in hand, and a British man relaxed in the hot water with a silver-haired woman, perhaps his wife. The woman stepped out of the pool from the side farthest away from Viduna, but the bald British man, in his pompous way, his shoulders thrown back with arrogance, swam all the way over to her side and got out, as if to make sure she noticed his hairy chest and his bulging swimming trunks. As he emerged from the water onto the ledge around the pool, his lean arms dripping, he said in a domineering tone, You'll get better light for reading at the deeper end.

Have a good night, she said when they finally left. The man returned a few minutes later, and she wondered whether she could get money out of him somehow. She smiled, and he leered at her. Maybe he and his wife were swingers. She thought about how that might work; the wife probably wouldn't be willing to spend on her.

He told her he'd left his steel water bottle on the other side of the pool, and evidently hoped she would swim over and get it, even though she was immersed in the Henry Miller. You're really not going to get it? he asked her in a nasty tone, as if he was shocked at how rude she was.

You're doing fine, she said, realizing with a sigh that no amount of charm would work to get him to like her enough to part with his money. After a long pause, he walked along the top edge of the basking pool to get it himself.

It's safe, really, he said, and stepped off the ledge as he reached the water bottle, pretending to fall off the cliff next to the infinity edge, even though there was a hidden promontory where he was stepping. She wondered how his wife or mistress or whoever that was telling him to hurry up from the path behind the fence could even stand him. She scowled. He fled.

From over the fence, his words came to her, whining that the woman wouldn't swim over to the edge of the pool and fetch the water bottle: I got wet again.

Poor baby, she murmured as she returned to her book, thinking about the erotic tiles in the bathroom of the Henry Miller Library, and wondering if those acts depicted in the tiles were the acts this British man performed with the demure woman to whom he was pathetically complaining.

But beggars can't be choosers, she reminds herself now, thinking that she needs to work on finding the next man.

Alone by the pool, she considers that the woman fog catcher who smirked at her in the bathroom had done so for some reason other than being in cahoots with Dariush. In the darkness of the patio, she feels someone might be lurking unseen, someone ready to attack. The baby hairs all over her body bristle with fear. She disrobes and steps one foot into the pool. Its heat is almost blinding, but she places her other foot in too. Over the infinity edge is the precipitous drop into an abyss of enormous clouds and fog.

She hears the voices before she sees them. Fog catchers. She recognizes their voices. Little Brown Braids. The Winking Woman. A nondescript bald man, older with a gaunt face. Hollow cheekbones, like an oil painting featuring a diner lit blue. There are two others, but she can't remember them.

They open the gate and wander toward the basking pool area, holding their heavy hiking backpacks, full of bottles of fog, to judge by the clinking.

Hello, she says, ignoring her uneasiness.

Little Brown Braids nods at her and looks at his companions. They set down their packs. He takes off his shirt and pants and enters the basking pool in his boxers. The opening in his boxers keeps widening. The man with the hollow cheekbones does the same. The two other men follow. Only the woman enters fully clothed. They watch Viduna as if trying to figure out what to say.

You're gathering fog, she says. She immediately feels dumb for stating the obvious, but the woman smiles. Her smile is lopsided.

What happened with that guy, your friend, that politician you were having dinner with? the Winking Woman asks.

Dariush? I don't know him.

Y'all sure seemed like friends, Little Brown Braids says. He doesn't make eye contact. He has a drawl, but it's an affectation, she realizes.

The other men laugh appreciatively. The Winking Woman tilts her head, like she's sizing Viduna up, trying to figure out whether she can take Viduna or not.

They occupy half the basking pool. She is just one alone on the other side of the small pool. Through the flood of hot white light, through the obfuscation of the steam and the clouds and the fog, they could descend on her. They look like they want to eat her; they look at her the same way Dariush did.

She asks, What are you going to do with all that fog in the jars?

The fog catchers look at each other, burbling with low laughter.

We sell it, the hollow-cheeked man says.

What, at a swap meet? She's picturing again what she imagined a few hours before.

You might say that, Little Brown Braids says slowly. 'S worth a lot over the mountains, inland.

A lot's worth a lot, the hollow-cheeked man says. We had to move there because of you rich people coming out to the coast after the seawalls were put up.

C-walls? She stands up, self-conscious in her pink bathing suit.

You going to that man's room now? the Winking Woman asks, simpering, knowingly, her eyes watery. He was *hot*, wasn't he?

You could tell she thought so, says the hollow-cheeked man.

No, I told you I don't know that guy.

They all laugh again.

Seriously, she says. Do you know him? Is that why you're interested?

They laugh.

Who are you? she asks irritably. They burst into peals of laughter.

She steps out of the pool and walks backward to her robe on the brown lounging chair, afraid they might stab her in the back if she turns away from them. They keep laughing as she puts her robe on, the force of their laughter somehow never shading into falsity even after she's made her way onto the path.

Clouds shift quickly. Stars break through patches of night sky cleared of fog. Low and mournful, frogs croak somewhere on the property, from the direction of the hillside. She hurries back to her room and fumbles with her key at the doorstep, looking over her shoulder, expecting either Dariush or the fog catchers. Only darkness behind her. She strains her ears, in case of a stealth attack.

Inside her room, she drinks some white wine from the minibar. As she relaxes, she wonders if Dariush was only offering something fun, light, and she misread things, interpreting similarities between him and the fog catchers. How paranoid she's been. She looks for the keys and slips a Klonopin into her pocket, in case of insomnia, and heads back onto the dark path, its edges obliterated by fog, which also obscures the redwoods that separate her from the clouds a thousand feet above the Pacific, the abyss into which she could easily fall.

He said the Ocean Room and she remembers seeing the sign for it closer to the restaurant. She pauses at each sign to decipher its words through the fog. Sounds filter through the white billows. Laughter, an eerie tone. The fog catchers. Anxiety dampens her armpits, though surely if she can't see them, they can't see her. Finally, in the midst of all the whiteness, she finds the wooden sign: Ocean Room. There. There is the light next to his door, just like the one next to her door, its yellow luminosity so strong it breaks through the white cover. She blunders through what feels like long wisps of cloud and arrives on the doorstep, where she stands trying to decide whether to knock or press the doorbell. She works up the courage and knocks, not too loudly, to give him the chance to ignore it. He opens the door just as she's turning away.

You came? He rubs his eyes like he might be imagining things.

She steps forward. He grabs her by the wrists and pulls her in. There is a surging in her heart, and it's desire, not fear. The room is more spacious than hers, with an enormous window through which nothing swirls, nothing there but white. He pulls her close and kisses her, leaves her breathless as he slowly pulls off her sweater, slides the skirt off her hips. His hands running along her hips, linger at the place where the bones thrust out and he leads a finger into her first. She feels herself liquid, throbbing.

IN THE MORNING IN the large room, Viduna wakes to fog, but it's inside her mind. A Klonopin hangover. Though it's early, Dariush is nowhere in sight. Hello? she calls into the half-light. She places her palm on the side of the bed where he fell asleep: cold. She pulls on her underwear. Hello? she calls again. Her dress, her sweater. No trace of him.

She returns to her room, mildly disturbed. After showering and changing clothes, she goes to the restaurant for coffee and breakfast at the buffet before checking out. To her surprise, a police car is parked along the path. A cop stands next to the car, drinking coffee from a paper cup and looking at his phone. She swallows her fear.

What's going on?

He tells her there's been an incident in the library.

What kind of incident?

A violent one, but I can't say more than that. He glances toward the Ocean House. Through the windows, she sees police officers where she'd been undressed last night.

She continues to the restaurant through the mist, shivering, her cardigan not thick enough to guard against the chill. In the restaurant, the waiters look anxious. She piles her plate with bacon and eggs. She pours coffee into a ceramic cup, finds a table, and gazes through the enormous windows at the cloud cover.

Everything okay? she asks the ginger-haired server who comes over to refill her coffee.

He smiles, pouring the coffee and not saying anything. Then, as if he can't help but dish, he whispers in a conspiratorial tone, There was a murder! The first ever on this property.

Viduna tries not to let her shock show, the better to obtain more information. A guest? Yes, maybe you met him? The Middle Eastern gentleman? Works with the government on solutions for the coast? The server is watching her face, like he already knows the answer. She tries to stay calm.

Oh, yes, I did meet him. What happened?

He was stabbed in the back five times walking down the path early this morning.

I'm so sorry to hear that, Viduna says, numb, thinking about Dariush's curious, intelligent eyes, how he'd entered her more slowly than she would have expected, based on the way he'd intruded on her space earlier in the restaurant.

Nobody can leave. The cops need to question everyone.

I have an audition scheduled in L.A. tomorrow, I have to head down.

The server shakes his head. You can't.

What happened to the fog catchers?

The server looks puzzled. Fog catchers?

You know that group that was here drinking house wine? They set a bunch of jars on the table?

They left the property after drinking, I believe. I don't remember anything about jars.

But I saw them in the basking pool a few hours after they were in here.

The server nods, as if he's simply going along with her to be polite, vacancy in his eyes.

AFTER BREAKFAST, SHE WANDERS the grounds, searching for the fog catchers, hoping to question them. She sees the body loaded into an ambulance after forensics is dispatched to the library. A row of quails, the first plump and matronly, the rest merely miniatures, crosses the path before her. Fog catchers—nowhere to be seen, but here comes more fog. Ever-present, constant, yet mysterious, and in the white plumes of fog, the salty taste of ocean, any sea creatures within it only the size of microns. Clouds thicker even than they were yesterday. Higher, closer to the precipice of the cliff. Seductive. They look thick enough to catch her if she were to walk off the cliff into them, and she wanders off the path toward the edge, slipping between the giant, unrelenting redwoods, careful not to go too far. Always the treacherous ocean, the ocean swirling and crashing far below, full of suicidal promise.

LATER, WHEN THE POLICE question her—the waiter revealed she was at his table the night before—Viduna can't quite remember the details of yesterday. They've already started to fade, time wearing them down, eroded by the steam coming off the basking pool, by the fearsome sight of the police car in the fog on the concrete path, by her own ceaseless return to the conversation with Dariush. She can no longer remember what they said, only how she felt. She doesn't explain her attraction to him, or how quickly it waned, then surged up again, threatening to overwhelm her in the room.

You should be asking the fog catchers, she insists to the detective. He looks at her like she's insane.

The people with jars of fog, who came over the hillside? They were in the restaurant last night, and after that, in the basking pool too. It was probably them.

Nobody else has mentioned them, says the cop to dismiss her, or perhaps to keep something from her. There's a guarded look in his eyes, and he makes a call, asking for a team to be sent out to talk to a witness, which she realizes with a start, is her.

We had a whole conversation. They asked me something about Dariush.

What did they ask you?

They'd been watching us eat dinner and wanted to know if I'd be going to his room after.

What did you say?

No. Of course, I said no.

She doesn't say anything about returning to Dariush's room, certain that will make her a suspect. The last thing she needs is to get any more caught up in this investigation, have them dig through her past, find out how many men she's swindled. She understands there's a difference between a confidence game and murder, but maybe they won't.

Was that before or after you took the Klonopin? How many did you say you took?

More clean-cut detectives arrive, and the questioning—that began when the sun was still at its midway point—lasts the remainder of the day. It is ceaseless, each question stranger and more specific than the last, many of them about the fog catchers, the basking pool, whether they'd talked about action to bring down the government, whether they'd shared their plans to preserve the coastline. They don't believe her, she can tell, though they seem to know everything about the fog catchers that the first detective pretended not to know about, and at the end of the interrogation, they ask her to stay another night, in case there are follow-up questions the next morning. The concierge advises her that any required extra nights will be complimentary.

Even after the interview is over, and she's surreptitiously walked past the library, squeezing through an area under construction to reach Billy's Trail, hikes through the looming redwoods to Lucie's Trail, and eventually makes it past the quiet yoga yurt, she continues to ask herself all the questions the detective did not. Why hadn't she gone back with Dariush right away? She saw from the detective's eyes, he hadn't quite believed her. Her talk of fog catchers at the basking pool immediately rendered her claims suspect. Who wandered the hillside catching fog in jars? Nobody. And when she talked about how they sold the jars at swap meets, the detective's eyes clouded with even more doubt. She said she went to sleep, omitting going back to Dariush's room, and he asked a few times whether she went right to sleep. Yes, yes, she answered, not sure what was giving her away. Had they done forensics on the room? Had she left something behind?

The sun never emerges in full force, never burns off the fog. As she wanders by the garden, she sees them up on the main road, five fog catchers talking loudly and laughing. Still on the property. Hey! she shouts. Hey! She needs to lead them back to the detectives to prove that she is not insane—everything that happened at the basking pool was real.

One turns and looks down at her, and the five break into a run, climbing up the concrete road.

She chases them, but they are far quicker than she is. As she nears the road, a deer with antler nubs darts out in front of her. She stops, bends over, out of breath, letting out a gigantic, painful moan at the stitch in her side. The deer stares at her before continuing down the hill.

The band of fog catchers, their bodies lither than she would have imagined, disappear over the crest of the hill.

SHE RETURNS TO THE restaurant the next morning. They haven't figured out who killed Dariush but suspect it was someone against the work he was doing for the government, and they've asked every guest to stay indefinitely—or rather announced that the guests will be doing so.

Any suspects yet? she asks the ginger-haired waiter.

He shakes his head. His eyes are shuttered, and she wonders if he suspects her.

You do remember the fog catchers after all, don't you?

Who?

The group that was here the other day with the bottles of fog. We saw you take their order.

She jerks her thumb at the table where they were sitting.

He murmurs a sound of amusement. Bottles of fog? Like I told you, I don't remember bottles of fog. Wine, maybe, but everyone orders that.

You have to remember, she insists. It was probably one of them that attacked Dariush. They were acting so strange at the basking pool that night. They're the ones the detectives should investigate. And they're out there! Yesterday, they were on the hillside running toward the last beach. I saw them.

Perplexed, his eyebrows knit together.

You really don't remember them?

The basking pool was closed that night.

Then how did I get in?

Did you hop the fence? His voice is stern.

Full of a dread she can't name, she looks away and asks to sit at the same table she sat at the night when she met Dariush, and once seated, she turns her body ever so slightly in the direction of Dariush's table. The ghostly gleaming disk of sun is at the same level as the top of the cliff, which she can see through the window. What might have happened had she treated him as a mark, had she invited him back to her room?

Stupid! So fucking stupid of her to sleep with him at all when she already assessed there were no prospects of a successful con.

She remembers only flashes of being with Dariush. Warm skin on skin. Breath. A surging inside her, a staggering release. Him falling asleep first. Her taking the Klonopin, losing all consciousness. Morning.

A man comes into the restaurant, and she looks up, certain that the body that was here, alive, that night, will be here again. There's something implausible about life suddenly being extinguished, and yet. The restaurant is alive with chatter, everyone trapped here indefinitely in familiar colloquies.

The fog catchers do not come. Dariush doesn't come. She's filled with longing for another timeline. One in which she invited him to her room. One in which she is not alone here in a series of tomorrow mornings, eating oysters, slippery, firm, and yet squishy, too, the taste of the sea as fog slips into the present moment, ready to disappear everything she remembers.

MOTHER, MY MONSTER

WHEN HE FIRST ARRIVED THAT autumn, Monster was dark and small. He burrowed into the tender crannies of his new home, shifting tissue, an errant squatter assiduously lodging himself away from the wildfires that burned outside. And he was not merely one but multifarious, and each of his many forms was monstrous, but a little different. Each of the folds of Mother's brain, a roller coaster. He played hide-and-seek in the gray crevices. Pleasure palpable.

At first, Mother didn't notice the trespasser. Monster stayed quiet, speechless, so as not to disturb her and arouse attention. This is how monsters marry their hosts.

A few months passed, Monster interfering with all the signals. He triggered a sleepy roll of fatigue, a fog rolling into every lit recess of Mother's mind, turning it dark. And Mother wanted to rest, to sleep.

Meanwhile, outside Mother's body, the baby crawled through the smoky world. Mother delighted in all the movement, in the way the light and shadows of the living room patterned the baby's face and romper. Quixotic smiles. Cooing. Monster watched, growing stronger, faster. The thin grasping hands of the clock traveled forward slowly, a series of ticks to engrave the passage of time, and as time grew deeper, both baby and Monster grew.

And in what seemed like a blink, it was autumn again, and Mother was pregnant with another baby, and Monster's power was shrinking. It wasn't clear what was happening because Monster's forms continued to ride the folds of the brain, reshaping them. Monster felt energy leaching away, slowly disappearing, as if each of his forms had been irradiated by the developing baby. Almost immediately after Mother birthed that baby, she became pregnant with another baby. And with this baby, the forms disappeared, and Monster breathed a tremendous sigh of longing. Mother had been a comfortable place to inhabit, but the baby, eating and cooing in her womb, seemed to take everything Mother had to offer, everything of the self that Monster had liked. Far away in her brain, Monster wondered what it would be like to be inside Mother's expanding bulge in this other way. Cared for, loved.

The new baby was birthed, and the baby and his two older sisters grew, as the years slid by, one after the other, the tick and the tock of them, the chime of the grandfather clock at every hour. Monster observed Mother unaware of the hours passing, too busy watching with pleasure as her babies toddled up and down the stairs.

And Mother didn't notice not noticing the time either, even though the time between wildfires grew shorter and shorter. Only every once in a while did Mother have clear days, and on those days, while everybody else huddled in their houses, afraid of the pandemic, the babies raced one another on their scooters around the driveway and illuminated the black, porous asphalt with fat pastel chalks. Monster thought he glimpsed himself in the little girl's portrait as if she knew what her mother didn't—that because of Monster, Mother had developed blank spaces where her memories had once been. The little girl represented those blanks with dark spots of asphalt in a swirling gold-and-orange scribble of fire, but of course, he couldn't say anything, couldn't pat her on the back and tell her she did a good job noticing his diligent work remaking Mother's mind. A pity.

His mission was a silent one. Silence is never the posture of the weak; it's the strategy of the strong and wily. Monster gained strength and power as Mother, his gracious host, sat in the sunlight, watching the children grow.

And Monster watched as Mother visited men in white coats, puny and terrifying in their human desire to know, to search him out, to sight his presence in the fog of her mind. They paid her complaints no mind, and Monster smiled. But as time passed, the semaphores led to Monster being spotted in all his many forms, his glory instantiated here and here and here and here. The men in white coats examined the forms it took on her brain and on her spine, and plotted Monster's defeat. Of course, the war having been mounted long before, and with his battle strategy plotted out long before they'd gotten there, the men in white coats were starting from a position of weakness. And Monster had a home-court advantage; he was inside and they were outside, not knowing much either about him or about Mother's brain.

Still, the men in white coats were armed with needles and slowed the multiplication of the monster while making Mother weaker too. He couldn't reproduce himself as quickly as he had before. No more roller coaster rides, no more moving tissue this way and that, snapping electrical signals, carefully loving and destroying the mother. Monster smiled to himself. He knew any defeat was only temporary. From the moment he'd trespassed, he'd had Mother in his clutches. Eventually,

he would fell her, and his darkness, ever so strong, would suf-
fuse her entire body, take residence in every cell of her brain
and spine, until she was crumpled, on her knees, in his thrall.

Years passed this way, Mother and Monster becoming,
not friends, but familiars—on intimate footing. Monster tap-
danced up and down Mother's spine, his every form finding
new ways to wreak mischief. And Mother learned to accept
Monster's presence, even as she continued to visit the men in
white coats, as they were, over time, her only hope at prevent-
ing the monster from loving her to death.

Mother's children grew, too, taller and wider and limbs
loose and rangy with joy. Monster came to feel Mother and
her children were his kin. Soccer tournaments and birthday
parties, children's theater and science fairs. Most of the time,
Monster kept Mother at home. She would be happier there at
home, resting. And if Monster noticed Mother crying from ex-
haustion or prostrate on the bed, wishing it would just be over,
if Monster noticed how Mother clutched her face at the cold
and pain efflorescing there, or startled at nimble electric pain
rushing her spine or the surging sensation in her legs—the
sensation that her legs were both being squeezed too hard—
if Monster noticed Mother needed a wheelchair and began
shaking, Monster didn't feel he needed to relent or sympa-
thize. Only natural, he thought. And there were, in all these
years, both a kernel of horror and a kernel of joy, and these two
kernels sprouted and grew into vines that intertwined, until it
became impossible to disentangle them, to distinguish horror
from joy, to allow either to blossom in its entirety.

The children left, and left, and left. And Mother, alone in
her wheelchair, sat by the closed window. Her hands trembled,
and she couldn't quite remember where the children were.
Or even how to speak. Or swallow. But she watched the dry,

shaking maple leaves fall limply from the tree, as smoke obliterated stars. She was uncertain about what this might mean for her, as she watched it all burn down.

AMRITA

November 10, 20--

Dear K,

I write to you in the season of death from my perch next to the hospital window. Finches are eating seeds from a feeder hanging from the lowest branches of a barren sycamore. They hop around the edge of the bowl, their claws grasping tightly, entirely unaware of the drama inside these walls.

Have you been in a place like this? I suspect not. There is no way to open the windows. I can't breathe in the ocean air that I know must be blowing in from the sea. This place is a void, no smells or textures to distinguish it from any other place. There are no locks on the doors, no security against the roving. I live in terror of the door bursting open; every hour the orderlies shove the door in, letting the knob bang the wall loudly, and, ignoring my fear, shout with cheerful authority, Just checking on you!

Every hour, imagine. You could go mad from that alone.

Just now in the sitting area, I watched a man lose it and get pinned by five beefy orderlies. He thrashed; they held his arms behind his back. Two hours before that in the dining room, a large frizzy-haired woman grew frustrated with all the restrictions, which she sees as excessive and arbitrary—she is right, though I know enough to keep that to myself—and began hurling her food across the room. One by one: eggs, muffin, bacon, plastic utensils, an opaque plastic cup of water sailed through the air. A few items hit other patients before landing and sliding across the speckled beige linoleum.

This is not a life. Before all this, I had a life. Perhaps you recall it, however faintly? I was on so many drugs—all sedating, all numbing, all a full-frontal attack on my memory—it's hard to remember much of that life. If I write it down here, maybe you can send the letters back to me when they let me out. You'll remind me, won't you? I'm counting on you to help me remember my past when it slips out of my reach.

Remember, earlier this autumn, I wrote to tell you I was working on something that would blow your mind? I could tell from your reply you didn't know what to make of that. All your hours phone-banking for this election that was so important to the country's survival, and I was going on week after week about some big personal secret.

Well, here is the secret: I've been formulating an elixir using ocean water and a secret molecule. My employers were not happy when they found out. The secret molecule was developed in their labs over many long hours. After all my colleagues went home, I stayed in the lab, combining and recombining molecules. Hours and hours stretching into each other, folding over on each other. Time is flexible. Inside its watery folds, there were many treasures to discover: the moon, a four-tusked elephant, a magic bow, devas and asuras, a tree that granted wishes.

I worked so many hours, I stopped sleeping. I was so sure this elixir would change the world. If only I dedicated myself completely, followed all my bright, ephemeral thoughts—their silvery rapidity, the spindrift cresting over them. God was working through me. I swear. Even so, it took a long time to figure it out. You might be wondering to what dream I pledged my devotion? I didn't want to tell you before because you never know who might intercept my letter, but that doesn't seem to matter anymore. Nothing does, and yet I need to pass my secret along to someone.

This elixir would allow us to live forever. No death. It wouldn't matter that I'm locked away in here for this tiny blip of time, because I would have all of eternity to make it up once I get out. Imagine the fantastical world we could build, if only we weren't haunted in every moment by our own decay.

Warmly,

A

November 13, 20--

Dear A,

Sorry to hear you've wound up in a psychiatric facility. I was concerned, I'll admit, when I read your letters from before. It became increasingly difficult to read them. Your sentences moved in tangents, like you were grooving on the disorder of your thoughts, and you stopped making sense, frankly. But I didn't know it was this bad, like hospital bad. How do we break you out of there? It must be terrifying. Though ... I'll be honest ... it also seems like it could be good for you. A place where you could sort yourself out and come back to earth. A place where you could be safe as all of society erupts into flames. A place that's safe. Other than the intrusive orderlies and people out of their minds, I mean.

My aunt never wound up in a place like that, but maybe she should have. And the medication is rough. I've seen what that did to her. The weight, the twitches. The way it pins down a thought, a butterfly, so it can never fly again. There can be too many thoughts, there can be too few: finding that balance with chemical intervention seems tricky.

Don't get upset, but immortality's not a dream of mine. I don't want to live forever. Do you? Do you really? It's enough to pay the bills, to be kind to each other. And our lives gain meaning from death, from how it approaches, whether slant or straight-on, the meaning is in traveling ever closer to it, the meaning is in how time twists and folds and squiggles as we move forward or sideways or even backward, but always approaching. As you say, time is flexible.

You can smell the cleansing sharpness of winter percolating through the air here. Soon, shaggy snow and ice hanging from pine. I'll be scraping ice from the car windows on my way to pick up the truck for work soon. Maybe when they release you, you can come visit me here in the Lou so we can finally see each other again in this lifetime.

Yours,

K

November 17, 20--

Dear K,

Do I detect skepticism in your letter? Perhaps you've already been defeated by social expectations: you don't want to live forever because you think you can't live forever. Perhaps your sense of possibilities is too narrow, shaped by constraints and rules entirely outside your control. All straight lines. No sense of the infinite. I can't live like that. I'm more interested in what happens when $y \neq mx + b$. How can you live a life so bounded, so circumscribed by the petty earthbound thoughts of other people, when you could be carousing with the stars?

I'm not sure when they'll let me out of here. They'll have to release me eventually, I think. They'll have to admit I'm not a danger to myself. Thanks for the invitation to St. Louis—maybe someday. I've been here a week now. Every day they ask me a battery of questions and say we'll revisit the question of leaving once I stabilize. I think what they mean is once I stop talking about the elixir. They don't understand that, even if I do stop talking about it, I'll still be thinking about what it might mean to live forever, to have an infinite amount of time to repair everything humans have put asunder on this earth. Not to have that ever-present deadline of death for all humans on this dying planet. I'll never stop thinking about what it means to live forever. It's my life's work.

My colleagues didn't understand either. They'd drive home to their spouses, their children, their Friday night movies, their weekend barbeques, their white picket fences, all the stuff they'd bought to counter their feelings of inadequacy, and they'd forget about the lab, the tests they'd run that had failed. They wanted to forget the daily letdowns of experiments, they wanted to live their lives, even though their lives were humdrum. You work too hard, they told me. And for what? You should take a vacation. Relax.

I smiled and nodded. Of course, they thought I should relax! I was getting ahead of them. They were half-assed and conventional in their ambitions. They wore blinders. They didn't see what I could see, how accelerating my experiments—failing faster every day—brought me closer and closer to the devas.

It started more than a month ago. I'd been walking on the beach by my townhouse early one morning watching the blush of sunrise when it came to me, this legend from the Puranas I'd heard in childhood. A sage gave Indra a garland as a gift and the god placed the garland on his elephant's trunk. When some bees buzzed by and irritated the elephant, he shook his big head and threw the garland onto the ground. The sage was furious at the disrespect and cursed all the devas. A battle between the devas and the asuras ensued. The asuras took over the universe but formed an alliance with the devas to churn the ocean of milk for a millennium to cook an elixir of immortality.

After I remembered the legend, I drove straight to the lab and I worked through the lunch hour, trying to figure out whether my vision could be realized. I went in over the weekends and stayed there, running tests, because I was sure if I tweaked the elixir ever so slightly, if I heated it to the right temperature, if I froze it, if I added poppy extract, if I added ephedra, I'd light upon the right formulation.

The last week before I wound up here was a blur.

I'd been on a long journey, battled demons, found the fourteenth treasure. And so I'd drunk some of the elixir, you see. Sweet and strange, but I couldn't see asking my employer to market it to the public if I weren't willing to try it myself first. I'm still not sure the elixir was entirely ready, though I know I was close, and I won't know for sure whether it works for years. If it does work, it won't matter if I'm in here a little longer. Two janitors found me that last Monday morning in the lab. I was sitting next to the door holding a beaker and babbling to myself, they said. Of course, they thought that: they don't know anything about science. It's all nonsense to them. Everything I said made sense if you knew what I know. Well, I don't want to tell you more if you're going to doubt me.

Sincerely,

A

November 21, 20--

Dear A,

Be honest, if I wrote to you from a psychiatric facility and told you about an elixir of immortality, you wouldn't believe me either. Nonetheless, I want to hear about it, this trip you've been on. I think I'll always be interested in what you have to say, even though it's been years since we've seen each other. Remember how we met on the cool stone steps outside the museum at the muggy lunch hour, both of us young and too broke to buy anything in the museum café, not able to afford more than a hot salty pretzel with cheap mustard from the cart propelled by the acne-covered vendor, watching the clogged traffic, the cars nosing ahead one by one, beneath the skyscrapers, beneath the tremendous clouds? How we spent the afternoon wandering through the halls looking at the paintings, at all the intensely personal iconography, the iconography of dreams made somehow eternally public. Klimt and Moreau and Redon. At twilight, a cloudburst, your address on a scrap of paper pressed into my damp, sweaty palm. It was one of the best days of my life. I was sure we'd meet again, and yet. All these missed chances to see each other since that cloudy afternoon. One day we'll meet again, I'm sure of it.

Forgive me my skepticism. I come by it honestly. My aunt would go on trips as well. She'd come back with a black eye, a broken rib, smelling of alcohol. She'd tongue the medication into her cheek, hiding whether she'd taken it. We couldn't monitor her every minute of every day. Forgive me my skepticism.

Yours,
K

November 30, 20--

Dear K,

I thought I might burn your letter to ashes. Were I not here locked away in this facility, I surely would have. Instead, I threw it in the trash and fumed. I'm only writing because you made me so angry, I spent the last week talking to you in my head, responding and responding and responding.

I don't think we'll see each other again. I am here and you are there. That day we met at the museum was nine fucking years ago and I'd just graduated college. The time we met up to go hiking in Yellowstone was seven years ago. Did I ever tell you I thought we might get together on that trip? But you were distracted, barely there. We talked about art and books and chemistry and physics, and your countenance kept falling, turning grim. On the last day, we were standing in a crowd, waiting for Old Faithful to blow, and I thought I might tell you how I felt, how I'd felt since I met you on those museum steps, but you started talking about geologic time in the play you were working on and asking me science questions, thinking I'd have answers because I'd just gotten my master's. And then the geyser erupted, all the hot white plumes shooting into the air, and we stood there awestruck, speechless, outside time. The moment to speak passed me by. When we said goodbye, you kissed me on the cheek. I wasn't sure we'd keep writing to each other, but a week later, your letter came, as it always did, as if you weren't aware of the moment at all.

Anyway, if you wanted to see me since then, you would have. If I'd wanted to see you, I would have. I don't know why we've bothered to keep in touch, to be honest. Is it to throw barbs at each other? Do you get a lot out of that?

Sincerely, but not warmly,

A

December 3, 20--

Dear A,

You cut me to the quick. Don't write me off. My letter wasn't intended as an incendiary. If I had the money to do so, I would have driven out to see you in the last few years. I was distracted at Yellowstone because I was worried about money, not sure whether I could afford to take the trip at all, anxious about the cost of the slice of cheesecake you wanted to split. If you weren't working around the clock at the lab, you probably would have flown out to see me between Yellowstone and now. I'm worried about you. Be honest, if you received a letter from me claiming to have invented an elixir of immortality, you'd question my sanity too.

Tell me. Tell me about the adventure of making this elixir. Why is it so important to you, locked away in a facility, that you live forever?

Yours,

K

December 6, 20--

Dear K,

I want to live forever because I want to live forever. I want to feel limitless, boundless. I don't want to die a vagrant, an itinerant, babbling on some dirty street corner one hundred miles from my home, alone and depressed and unable to escape my own theories about why America is the way it is. Before all this happened, I took a paranoid man to get a burger at McDonald's and he told me his conspiracy theories about the powerful in society, and they made a kind of sense to me. When I look at the people around me right now, the people society insists are my people, I see that dirty street corner's not at all a far-fetched possibility. I could be that man.

I want to be forever young, forever excited about life, never middle-aged and trapped and disappointed with how things turned out. The elixir would make that possible, no matter what my therapist says, peering at me from under her auburn bangs. I see her every morning for a one-on-one in this hellhole, and every morning she gently reminds me that the elixir is a delusion, that I can fight this delusion by taking control of my thoughts and accepting that certain thoughts are only thoughts flitting through my mind, and aren't necessarily true because I've thought them. Then she sends me off to an hour of art therapy to make collages that express my mood. And while I cut and glue those collages, scrapping together images of the legend from the Puranas that keeps coming back to me in fits and bursts, I wish I had more talent. But the thing is, I do have a talent and that talent is for making elixirs, not collages. If only other people knew.

Weeks have passed, and I still haven't made any friends here, and this, apparently, makes me unfit for discharge. But what if I'm the only one who is sane? I feel like their thoughts might be contagious, or maybe, more clearly, like I don't have the normal defenses against the onslaught of their thoughts. My only means of protection is to distance myself, to cocoon myself in thoughts of the elixir.

Again, today, a wisp of a young woman was pinned to the ground by guards. Like me, she is from South Asia, but from the North somewhere, I think, and she kept sitting next to me in the room with the TV and asking me questions in a fragile, vacant tone. Where did I live? What part of India was I from? When was I getting out? And I didn't want to answer because the familiar and intensifying waves of these queries made me uncomfortable, like we were the same. I needed a seawall to protect myself from her. But now I keep thinking of her defenseless, nose to the ground, vulnerable, trembling, not dangerous at all, with an enormous male orderly with his knee pinned against her back.

I don't want to think too long about the reality of that, of how people try to control and overpower one another, how fragile our shared reality is, how democracy in America has been falling apart for years, broken by the bullies of society and their quest for power and control—that knee of domination on a young woman's back—but the thought keeps slipping unbidden into my mind. I try to push it away by thinking about that day on the beach when all this started.

The memory of dark-blue waves lapping the pinkish, sunlit sands and, much farther out, the life puff of a whale's migration over the water, brings me peace. I'd been walking along the cliffside and found a garter snake. I picked it up and carried it with me to the edge of the sand. The snake told me to put him into the water. He stared at me with beady eyes. He told me to put his tail in the water and churn. I churned and I churned. Out of the water rose treasures. The churning was so strong, the mountain behind me was upended and moved slowly forward, slipping into the ocean. A giant tortoise emerged from the ocean and told me to take some of the spindrift and carry it back to the lab in my water bottle. I let go of the snake who was washed out to sea. I bent down and filled the bottle with salt water and drove back to the lab, traveling the happiness curve to a brighter future. That's the feeling I want, the feeling of infinity.

How do I find that feeling again? I won't find it in here.

Sincerely,

A

December 10, 20--

Dear A,

I suppose it might be easier to secure your release if you follow their rules? Nobody wants to live by other people's rules, but we all have to do it. I'd rather be at the ocean myself, but instead, I am here, inland, in one of the cheapest cities in the country. I wanted to be working on a play, and I'd thought I had a breakthrough, but instead, I had to phone-bank and work the polls because our country was going up in smoke. The candidate wasn't particularly amazing, but the only way we'll get the country we want is if we keep doing the work to put people into power who have hearts. I don't want to wake up at five in the morning to deliver furniture for a living, but how else will I keep the light on?

Here is what I never told you about that day at the museum. I sat down close to you on the steps on purpose. I knew straightaway that we would know each other for a long time. Who knows why I thought that. It was probably a delusion. But the thing about delusions is that you can make them come true sometimes. You looked at me and said something about the pretzel and street food. You said you'd had better on the streets of Mumbai. I was taken with you right away. Your ease with strangers. The sense that wherever you went would be home because you would make it so. That same expansive confidence, I fear, has you invested in an elixir that hasn't brought you much good. Whether immortality is a delusion or not—I know you think not—you don't want to waste away in there, do you? I hope you follow the rules, go to therapy, socialize with your fellow patients, so you can go home again.

If you manage to go home again, I promise I will come see you.

Yours,

K

December 13, 20--

Dear K,

You are right. Of course, you are. That day on the stone steps, I had no thoughts of immortality. I cared only for the moment, that one point in time, oblivious to all that was tangential to it. I didn't care much if death was around the corner because I was so thrilled to be there in the city. I just wanted to talk to that beautiful boy sitting nearby on the steps watching the traffic go by. The pretzel was a good excuse. We were both broke.

Immediately, I was absorbed in what you knew of the Symbolists. The stories you could tell about those artists, their obsessions. I fell for you, I think, while we were wandering through the museum, telling each other what we saw, as if the other were not there seeing it too. We interpreted for each other. We didn't see the same thing in any of those framed canvases. It was exciting in the moment, but I am thinking of it today because now, reading how little you think of my invention, I wonder if there was any connection there at all.

I followed your suggestion anyway. I've started socializing with my fellow patients. I do not talk about the elixir anymore in my therapy sessions, though this doesn't mean I don't think about it. My therapist says she'll let me out by next weekend if I keep up the good work and progress. I don't know if there's anything good in the world out there, though. The medication has slowed me down. I hate the way that it cuts the wings off my thoughts. There is no flying away on these drugs. It forces me to think I'm earthbound after all, no different from the others locked up here. I keep that in mind as I try to make friends.

There is an intimacy, us against the orderlies, but that's not fellowship, is it?

From the window, I watch the bird feeder, but the birds don't come back. I wonder if they've migrated like the whales do, if it's too cold for them, even here.

Sincerely,

A

December 16, 20--

Dear A,

Perhaps the birds flew here. When I look out my window, I see a flock of them sitting on the telephone wire, hanging out on the tree, gossiping to their hearts' content. I'm tempted to give one of them this letter and see if it returns to you. Do they allow you to open the windows and let some fresh air in over there? I'm glad, I can't say how glad, that you're doing your best to get released now.

That day on the steps: I wanted to impress you with those stories. I could see you were brilliant within the first five minutes. You terrified me. I was sure you'd see right through me and everything I was saying about the Symbolists. And if I'm honest, I was a little terrified by how quickly your mind worked. The thing is, you might feel slow, but you're probably now working at normal speed, like a mere mortal. There's nothing so wrong with that, is there? Being mortal, being alive?

Yours,

K

December 19, 20--

Dear K,

Everything is wrong.

It feels like I'm being dragged through quicksand. Time dragging me in its jaws. Nobody would want to live forever like this; plowing through this sludge of days, hours, minutes. Is this what having a normal brain feels like? All the magic drained out of everything? Every shape, every color a little dull, blunted, boring? I don't know how anyone could go on for an entire eighty years this way, much less all eternity. It's so disappointing! Don't you think so? That there's nothing spectacular in all of this, just atoms and molecules colliding. No crashes, no thrills, just this painfully ordinary, bounded life.

I'm never going to recapture that feeling of the day by the ocean, am I? It's gone forever. Nobody understands how beautiful that moment was with the snake and the water spiraling down in a whirlpool. The radiance of sunlight glinting off the ocean-slick head of the snake, the droplets hanging from its teeth. It was a mere flash of time. I'm expected to live on that brief ecstasy for the rest of my lonely minutes on this planet? It's too horrible for words.

Today is my last day in this facility. I tried to explain the beauty I'd glimpsed to the people in group this morning, but nobody understood. Their faces were blank, and there were no words that changed their expressions. Nobody is inside for the same reason. They'd been depressed, or they'd been mad, but none of them had been exuberantly so. They'd never had that pure feeling of being transported out of your body, the promise of eternity in the lip of a wave. They have always been bounded, I think, and they understand boundaries as worth the trouble. Or maybe language, that tool of sociability, simply

wasn't designed to match the blissed-out, tremendous feeling of standing outside society, outside everything, including
yourself. Maybe I'd be doubtful, too, if I hadn't seen the way
that churned ocean looked for myself.

I stopped trying to explain once I saw how they looked at
me. In disbelief. Smirking. Scowling. Medicated. Within these
four walls, walking around on this linoleum, you're supposed
to be suffering and slow, or agitated and angry. Nobody here
knows what to do with the inconvenience of euphoria, the way
it eludes all the words.

I have to pack to return home now. They're letting me out.
Finally.

I am half expecting they will change their minds and keep
me for further observation.

Sincerely,

A

December 22, 20--

Dear A,

Relieved to hear you are getting out after the past, what,
month? Has it been longer? Steep price to pay for a single moment of ecstasy, I'd say.

Don't take this the wrong way, but what if an ordinary life
were a dream worth more than you think? What if it were possible to have had that moment of ecstasy alongside all the ordinari-
ness of everyday living? The work of paying bills. The cleaning of
your house. The sweat of cold-calling, fundraising, trying to get
a decent candidate elected. The feeling of wriggling your toes at
the bottom of cool, clean sheets. The feeling of slicing open the
mail, not knowing what you might find. It might be implausible
in an opera to have that ecstasy and yet return to finding serenity

in the lowly ordinary, but that is your life. How stunning is that? You were able to have both in one life.

Maybe that one singular moment you had at the ocean is enough. Maybe—hear me out, don't burn this letter in anger—you don't need more.

Yours,

K

December 26, 20--

Dear K,

I walked to the ocean at daybreak today. There were no garden snakes, no gods or goddesses. It was freezing cold. The sky was overcast, muffling the gold line of the sun at the horizon. The ice plants looked subdued. Even the birds seemed chastened.

While I was walking up and down the sand, HR called me to let me know they are sending me all my effects by mail, so I shouldn't return to the lab. I emailed a few colleagues, but none responded, not even a sentence. They would eventually write, they would care what happened to me, wouldn't they? They didn't.

I didn't tell you this before because it was too humiliating and painful—my chest tightens so fiercely with despair I want to throw up just remembering it—but the janitors weren't the only ones who found me that Monday morning. After they called the ambulance, a number of my colleagues arrived and tried to calm me down. I can't remember what happened clearly. I told you I would forget. It's all dark shadows and strange angles of faces. Dark, angry eyes. Suspicion. My chest aches with the weight of seeing in their eyes who they thought I was: a threat. They thought I meant them harm. They didn't mean me well either, and I didn't know how to convince them I was safe because they didn't know what I was talking about. My language failing just as it would inside the facility. I was bedraggled, unkempt, unwashed, talking about a secret molecule, certain I could convince them of my delusions. I am left with their faces. When I think of their faces, I can't go on. How do I go on, left only with all of that wreckage? Tell me; I'm out of ideas.

Maybe I try to think so much about the ecstatic moment when I thought up the elixir of immortality in order to survive the loss of trust, the unshakable knowledge of how quickly fellowship can be undone, how quickly the people you ate lunch with and laughed with and worked with every day see you as a threat to their buttoned-up lives and would rather never speak to you again.

This life is so lonely.

Sincerely,

A

December 29, 20--

Dear A,

My aunt had experiences like that all her adult life, or at least I think she did. It's hard to know anything from the outside. As you say, the feelings elude language. Out of the blue, she would get happier and happier, a soul like a helium balloon, propelled upward. Flights of ideas that seemed to fit together, but not quite—angled speech—traveling along currents none of us could see. For weeks, she'd speak quickly. We couldn't follow her. She went somewhere we couldn't, though looking back, I'm not sure she could even follow herself. She didn't want to sleep. I always wondered what was happening in her mind.

Once or twice, we had to call the police to restrain her because her energy was unbelievable. She lost her job, and then she lost another one and another one. Her husband paid the mortgage until he died, but he left the marriage and the house. She lost all her friends. That was the saddest thing to witness. As years passed, they stopped checking on her, stopped calling. I tried to see things from their perspective, to understand how they could abandon her like that, but I couldn't. I was left only with judgment at their cruel apathy. When you have cancer, people bring roses and zinnias and daffodils, a whole kitchen full of flowers, but with this—eventually even her sons, my cousins, stopped checking on her. They went off to chase their ambitions, while she fell into catatonia. In her last cruel years, my parents, who lived down the street, were the only ones left to buy her groceries and pay the utilities. There was only so much they could do. She lived like a ghost alone in that big empty house in the suburbs, hoarding every scrap of paper, every knickknack, trying to keep alive the memory of being well as it receded further and further into the distant past, perpetually deciding that medication didn't help her, that it slowed her down too much. She never came out alive again.

But I don't believe for one second that had to happen, you know? Nothing is inevitable. She could have stayed on her medications, understood herself as simply a speck in history, made peace with the ordinary. You can too. And her friends! Her friends could have stayed and seen she was one of them, not merely her illness, in spite of what horrific thing had happened to her. They could have loved her.

I will be away for the next three or four days. You'll see soon enough why.

Yours,
K

January 10, 20--

Dear K,

I didn't expect to find you on my doorstep last week. Did I dream you up? Was that real? Please don't tell me if it wasn't.

I can't believe you drove out here to see me. You were as I'd remembered you. You haven't aged! Do you have a portrait of yourself in some dusty closet that reveals all your lines and wrinkles?

I hope I wasn't too much? There is such a thing, I know now, as a limit, a hard limit, even if it's invisible. You keep approaching, but you don't want to cross over. I crossed over. I don't want you to feel like you cross over when you're with me.

This is what I struggled with most in group. This mechanical way of talking about reality as entirely determined by society's expectations, this realization that to live among other humans, I need to want boundaries and limits that, in fact, I don't desire at all. Want suggesting lack, desire suggesting excitement. But I think you're right. I can't want that illusory moment by the ocean to last forever, at least I can't chase it and also respect the ordinary.

There is an asymptote to the happiness curve, I'm learning. I need to travel it, whether or not I'm ever going to quite get there. When you move out here, you'll travel it with me, won't you?

The ordinary is enough, I think.

Yours,

A

ACKNOWLEDGMENTS

Thank you to visionary editor, Peg Alford Pursell and WTAW Press, for believing in this book, as well as my last. To extraordinary publicist Beth Parker. To my agent Melissa Danaczko for her patience and much-appreciated advice.

To my dear comrades-in-arms Emily Holleman, Meghan Maguire, and Ina Roy Faderman, who were the earliest readers of these stories. To the Ruby for the space to work, and in particular, to these Rubies for being early readers: Katy Van Sant, Amber Butts, Suzanne Wang. To the pandemic writers' group: Chaya Bhuvaneswar, DeMisty Bellinger, Greg Marshall, Sarah Gonzalez, and Yohanca Delgado. To fellow writers for the sustenance of good conversations; invariably, they influenced this book: Ann Gelder, Lisa Teasley, Sarah Stone, Ron Nyren, and Elizabeth Gonzales James. For seeing me through everything, as always: Elisa Cheng, Athena Wong, Karin Spirn, Phoebe Kitanidis, Kerry Guinn, and Jo Greiner.

Much gratitude to the editors and literary magazine editors who gave these stories their first homes: Lisa Levine and *Terrain*; David L. Ulin and *Air/Light*; Blaise Zerega and *Alta Journal*, as well as Selected Shorts at Symphony Space for featuring the story; Lisa Locascio, Axel Wilhite, and *7x7*, along with collaborator Jody Zellen, who created the art that ran alongside an earlier version of "The Glitch"; Nicole Chung and *Catapult;*

Dorothy Rice and Shelley Blanton-Stroud and *TwentyTwenty: Stories on Stage Sacramento Anthology*; and Taylor Pavlik, Rebecca Rubenstein, and *Midnight Breakfast*.

To my loves Steven, Illyria, Kavi, Beckett, and my parents. Without you, none of these phantasms—nor the eked-out time to put them on the page during the early years of the pandemic— would be imaginable.

ABOUT THE AUTHOR

Anita Felicelli is the author of the novel *Chimerica* and the award-winning short story collection *Love Songs for a Lost Continent*. Her essays and criticism have appeared in the *Washington Post,* the *Los Angeles Times, Los Angeles Review of Books,* and the *New York Times* (Modern Love). Anita is the editor of *Alta Journal*'s California Book Club. From 2021-2024, she served on the board of the National Book Critics Circle. She lives in the San Francisco Bay Area with her family.

About WTAW

WTAW Press is a 501(c)(3) nonprofit publisher devoted to discovering and publishing enduring literary works of prose. WTAW publishes and champions a carefully curated list of titles across a range of genres (literary fiction, creative nonfiction, and prose that falls somewhere in between), subject matter, and perspectives.

WTAW Press provides discounts and auxiliary materials and services for readers. Ebooks are available for purchase at our website bookshop. Readers' guides are available for free download from our website. We offer special discounts for all orders of five or more books of one title.

Instructors may request examination copies of books they wish to consider for classroom use. If a school's bookstore has already placed an order for a title, a free desk copy is available. Please use department letterhead when requesting free books.

Author appearances, virtual or in-person, can often be arranged for book groups, classroom visits, symposia, book fairs, or other educational, literary, or book events.

As a nonprofit literary press, WTAW depends on the support of donors. We are grateful for the assistance we receive from organizations, foundations, and individuals. We especially wish to thank the following individuals for their sustained support.

Nancy Allen, Lauren Alwan, Robert Ayers, Andrea Barrett, Mary Bonina, Vanessa Bramlett, Harriet Chessman, Melissa Cistaro, Mari Coates, Kathleen Collison, Martha Conway, Michael Croft, Janet S. Crossen, R. Cathay Daniels, Ed Davis,

Walt Doll, DB Finnegan, Joan Frank, Helen Fremont, Nancy Garruba, Michelle Georga, Ellen Geohegan, Anne Germanacos and the Germanacos Foundation, Rebecca Godwin, Stephanie Graham, Catherine Grossman, Teresa Burns Gunther, Annie Guthrie, Katie Hafner, Christine Hale, Jo Haraf, Adrianne Harun, Lillian Howan, Yang Huang, Joanna Kalbus, Alice Kalman, Susan Keller, Caroline Kim-Brown, Scott Landers, Ksenija Lakovic, Evan Lavender-Smith, Jeffrey Leong, The Litt Family Foundation, Margot Livesey, Karen Llagas, Nancy Ludmerer, Kevin McIlvoy, Jean Mansen, Sebastian Matthews, Grace Dane Mazur, Kate Milliken, Barbara Moss, Scott Nadelson, Betty Joyce Nash, Miriam Ormae-Jarmer, Cynthia Phoel, John Philipp, Lee Prusik, Gail Reitano, Joan Silber, Charles Smith, Michael C. Smith, Marian Szczepanski, Kendra Tanacea, Karen Terrey, Renee Thompson, Peter Turchi, Genanne Walsh, Judy Walz, Tracy Winn, Rebecca Winterer, Heather Young, Rolf Yngve, Olga Zilberbourg

To find out more about our mission and publishing program, or to make a donation, please visit wtawpress.org.